FOR THE PLOT

Stone Siblings Book One

Emily B. Rose

PUG PRESS PUBLISHING

FOR THE PLOT

EMILY B. ROSE

FOR THE PLOT

Cover Design & Illustration: Gabby, @themoonborn

Chapter Header & Scene Break Design: Emily B Rose, @emilybrosewrites

This is for every person who ever felt they were "behind" because of some arbitrary social construct. Your relationships and experiences don't define you.

ALSO BY EMILY B ROSE

Call of the Sea Series
Call of the Sea

The Stone Siblings Series
For the Plot

AUTHOR'S NOTE

I want to start by saying thank you so much to every person who has picked up this book. It means more than I'll ever be able to express that you want to read my story about fat, queer, neurodiverse people falling in love. I want to mention a few things about this book before you dive in.

Bof the main characters in *For the Plot* are demisexual and bisexual. One of the things I wanted to explore with this book is how different people experience demisexuality differently. Demisexuality, like every other sexual orientation, is a spectrum, and no two people's experiences will be exactly the same. This book is written from one single demisexual person's feelings and experiences. If this is not how you experience demisexuality, that's OK!

Also a reminder that Nikki is also fat, and has ADHD and deals with depression. James is mid-size and deals with chronic gastritis. These representations are based on my own experiences with fatness, ADHD, depression, and chronic gastritis.

content warnings

For the Plot features on page explicit sexual content be–tween two consenting adults. In one scene, they engage in explicitly consensual sex while under the influence of marijuana.

There are also on page descriptions of a depressive episode, alcohol consumption, and internal thoughts of previous body image issues.

STONE FAMILY TREE

LAURA STONE (51) + PETER STONE (52)

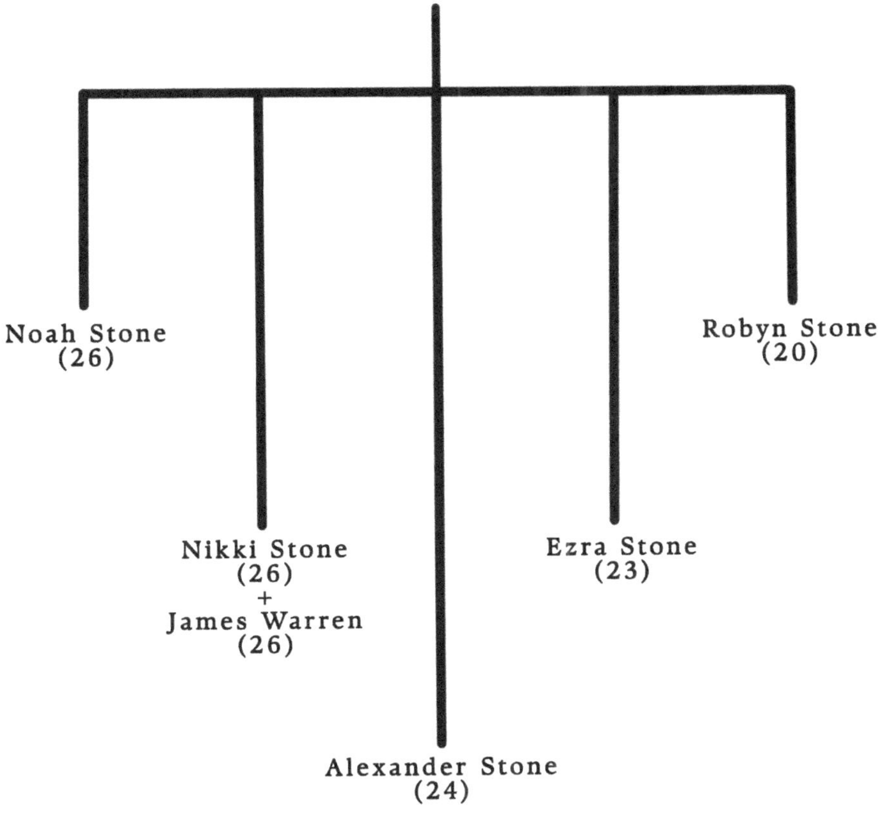

Noah Stone
(26)

Nikki Stone
(26)
+
James Warren
(26)

Alexander Stone
(24)

Ezra Stone
(23)

Robyn Stone
(20)

1

NIKKI

"You taste so good," his voice purred as his body pushed hers up against the wall.

Ugh, purred? Really? What was he, a fucking cat? *Delete, delete, delete.*

I dropped my hands from the keyboard, banging my head onto the desk in front of me. I couldn't remember the last time it had been this hard to find words that sounded right. Or even to find words at all. Usually, they flowed out of me, a never-ending, hyperfixated stream. Sure, they were pretty messy the first go-round, but they were always *there.*

Until the one thing I had been terrified of for the past two years finally happened. Until I had been outed as a fraud.

No, I chastised myself. I wasn't a fraud, and my brain needed to stop being so mean. I just...

I groaned in frustration, deciding I had tortured myself enough for one evening, shutting my laptop with a decisive *snick.* Pushing as far away from my desk as my messy clothes strewn floor allowed, I got up and stretched out the pain from my shoulders.

Normally I couldn't sit in the same position for longer than five seconds at any given time. But when I got into a hyperfocus, time ceased to exist. I'd lost whole hours, entire *days,* before, so focused on whatever was in front of me. Sometimes it was a productive focus—but most times, it was definitely not. Like the time I decided to finally clean my room top to bottom. One hour in, I got sidetracked reading through my old journals and trying not to cringe too hard at my teenage angst, just to look up what felt like moments later to find the sun had actually gone down hours before.

This was not one of those times. I sat down to start writing three hours ago, and the line I deleted was as far as I had gotten—a.k.a., exactly nowhere. It had been like this since The Review.

The book I was writing—supposedly writing, that is—was my third book. And of course, the first two had been hard. So hard I felt like quitting every other minute, pulled out what felt like half my hair, and cried my body weight in tears, which at my size, was a lot of fucking tears.

Yet, I *had* written them. I had been able to finish those drafts and submit them to my editor, even if it nearly killed me each time. But now? My deadline was *last* week, and I was still less than halfway through the book.

And that deadline had been pushed back from the one three months prior.

Which was three months after the *first* deadline had been.

God, I was so fucked.

I didn't even want to open my bank app and see what my account had dwindled down to.

Before I could spiral even further, my phone began ringing. I looked around the mess of half-full cups and empty chip bags on my desk until I eventually found it half buried under the pajamas I had thrown off this morning in exchange for more appropriate working clothes. And since I worked from my bedroom, that meant a soft cropped T-shirt and the baggiest pair of sweatpants I owned. Who willingly wore real pants at home? I shuddered at the thought.

Remembering that I was supposed to answer the call *before* it stopped ringing, I hastily swiped across the screen without even checking who the caller was.

"Nikki!" The voice on the other end sounded pleasantly surprised, and I quietly cursed my own stupidity. Listen, my agent Lucy was incredible. I was so beyond lucky to have them on my team, and I couldn't imagine a better person in my corner. But I also looked up to them so much, and I hated disappointing them. Which was all it felt like I was doing lately, as exemplified by the fact that they sounded surprised that I'd even picked up their call.

I truly was the worst.

"Lucy! Hey, it's good to hear from you!" My voice sounded high-pitched even to my own ears. I had nothing good to tell Lucy, and I knew this call was not going to be a fun one for either of us. Hence why I had been avoiding their calls for the last week. Six days to be exact. The first call I ignored was the day my draft had been due, and all I sent was an email to Lucy and my editor that the draft wasn't ready and that I needed a little more time.

"You've been avoiding me, haven't you?" Their wry voice cut through my internal thoughts, and I focused back on the conversation at hand.

"Psh." My mouth moved before my brain could catch up long enough to stop it. "I have no idea what you mean." I slapped my hand to my forehead, flinching as it made a loud smack, definitely loud enough to be heard through the phone pressed against my ear.

Lucy sighed in response. "Listen, Nikki, I get it, okay? No one likes getting bad reviews." I huffed in derision at that gross understatement. "But you need to get back on track, sweetie. You know I love you and I've got your back, but you've already pushed this deadline twice. Your sales are good, but they're not 'I can push back deadlines indefinitely because my publisher can't afford to lose me' good."

I flopped back onto my mattress, putting the phone on speaker and tossing it next to me as I stared up at the ceiling. "I know," I reluctantly started. "I know, and I swear I'm working on it. That's actually what I was doing when you called."

I hated how quickly their voice perked up. "Really? And how far have you gotten?"

Wincing, I tried to decide how honest to be. It's not like they wouldn't figure it out when I sent them a big old draft of nothing. "Well..." I began, but they cut me off, their Nikki bullshit detector 100% accurate.

"Listen, Nikki." Lucy's voice was kind, but firm. And this was one of the many reasons I had known they were the right agent for me. We just clicked, and we genuinely enjoyed each other. Not to mention the fact that they're queer and understood me on that level. And, well, they were really good at putting me in my place and not letting me get away with my shit. I'm a twenty-six year old woman with late-diagnosed inattentive ADHD. If there is no external pressure for me to do something? Yeah, that's never getting done. "I will go back to your editor and ask for another extension. But I don't know what she's going to say."

I'm pretty sure I knew. I was a mid-list romance author in an oversaturated genre, with no wildly viral books or huge social media followings, and only a two-book backlist to my name. My position was in absolutely no way secure. Not to mention the next segment of my advance only came once I submitted the final book under my three-book contract, and I was very quickly running out of money. I'd probably be out by the end of the year. "I swear, Lucy, I'm trying." I pressed the palms of my hands into my eyes until little stars popped up in my vision and hoped Lucy couldn't hear the wobble in my voice. I swear, all I ever did was try, and it never felt like enough.

Lucy's voice softened. "Oh sweetie, I know you are. How much do you have left to write?"

I mumbled my response.

"Nikki…"

Sighing, I sat up, picking the phone back up and taking it off speaker. "I'm still not at the halfway mark."

There was silence on the other end, and I pulled it away to make sure the call hadn't dropped. "Lucy?" I asked timidly, afraid this might be what finally made them lose all faith in me.

"I'm here." Their voice was reassuring, but distracted. Sure enough, I could hear the keys of their laptop clicking away, and I was sure if this was an in-person conversation, I would see the tip of their tongue poking from the corner of their mouth. "Sorry, I'm trying to get ahead of this. I will do my best to get you another extension. In the meantime, I need *you* to figure out how to get yourself past this mental block. I don't care what it takes—take up yoga or rock climbing, start meditating, learn how to surf, whatever. Hell, buy yourself a new vibrator. Anything you can think of to get your mind moving enough to keep writing."

A grin spread across my face at the exasperation seeping into Lucy's voice by the end, their vibrator recommendation nearly making me choke on my laughter. I shot a look at my nightstand out of the corner of my eye. Yeah, I got that one covered already.

"Alright, I promise. I'll think of something."

The clicking stopped on Lucy's end, and their voice came back more clearly. "We'll get through this, Nikki. Ride or die, baby. We're in this together."

I finally felt like smiling, really smiling, for the first time in days. "We're in this together," I repeated back, half to them and half to remind myself.

We ended the call, and I stared at the wall, my mind spinning with ideas of what I could do to get myself out of this rut. Because if I didn't get out of it… I had been surviving on the first segments of my advance from my earlier book, and if I didn't get the next portion I would receive once this manuscript was turned in and accepted, I was going to run out of money. My roommates were great, but none of them could afford to pay my portion of the rent, and I would never ask them to do that. And I refused to go back to my parents and ask them for rent money, or even worse, if I could move back in.

No, if I ran out of money I would have to look for another job, and with the job market as hard as it was, that was going to be nearly impossible. And I knew myself. I would burn myself out in two seconds flat attempting to work a job and continue writing. Which meant that I had no choice. I *had* to figure out how to get out of this slump.

But I groaned in frustration when the thoughts started spiraling faster than I could process, only stressing me out even more. Normally, I could brush off the negative reviews when I stumbled across them. You can't please everyone, and as much as it killed my people-pleasing soul, even I knew that.

But how the hell was I supposed to get over the reviews saying my sex scenes sounded like they were written by someone who's never had sex... when it was true?

2

NIKKI

YMCA - Village People

I HADN'T MEANT TO lie, not really. It had just kind of... happened. More like an omission than a lie. Was I supposed to just announce my sexless status? It wasn't like the whole world was entitled to hear about my sex life, or lack thereof. Being a romance author who writes smut could be a mindfuck sometimes.

I considered myself a sex-positive person. I loved promoting depictions of healthy sexuality, and was a firm believer in destigmatizing discussions around sex. But I was also an incredibly awkward human being who had *never* been comfortable talking about sex growing up, even with my friends. I didn't have an issue talking about sexuality or even my (lack of a) sex life when it was all hypothetical. But when it came to the actual thing—being physically intimate, even platonically—I always froze. It was just how I had always been.

In high school while all my friends began falling in love and lust, I just... didn't. For a long time, I wondered if maybe something was wrong with me. Maybe something inside me was broken if I didn't feel the same way all my peers, including my twin sister, seemed to. But then again, I was always falling in love with fictional characters. And I did want a partner. I craved the affection and emotional intimacy I saw in my friend's relationships, the casual touches and looks, the warmth of being wanted and chosen. When I got older, I went on a few dates through a dating app, even kissed some people, and had one mediocre attempt at a hookup, but nothing had ever felt *right*. The desire for sexual intimacy just didn't seem to come to me the same way it did for everyone else.

And then in my freshman year of college, I realized that yeah, I did want the sexual intimacy as well. I had just never felt safe enough to explore that part of myself until I read my first smutty romance book and my whole world changed.

That was when I discovered the term demisexuality, from one of the romance books I read. It felt like that piece inside of me that had always been just a little off finally clicked into place with that label. Only feeling sexual attraction for someone after an emotional connection—that was *me.*

Suddenly, it made sense why I always fell in love with fictional characters, but had never fallen in love in real life. With a fictional character, you got to know them, their deepest darkest thoughts and fears, their every internal thought. What was more intimate than that?

And with romance books in particular, the way I could dive into a character's head, feel their sexual desire as if it was my own? Paired with my obsessive tendencies, I was gone. I devoured romance book after romance book, until I was so entrenched in the genre I just had to write my own. I never even planned to be an author, let alone a romance author. It was more like fate, or destiny.

I graduated with my degree in communications, entered the bullshit world of capitalistic hell, and barely made ends meet in my underpaid, overworked retail job. But at night, I had the smutty little stories I was writing to bring me joy and make me feel less alone.

And then Noah, my twin sister, convinced me that I should try to get it published. The asshole snuck onto my computer and read the book I was working on without telling me. At first, I was embarrassed that my twin sister read the sex scenes I wrote. But she just told me how good the story was and convinced me that I should go for it.

And somehow I did. And then I got an agent. And then suddenly I was quitting my day job because I had just gotten a three-book deal for a romance series about three best friends finding their happily-ever-afters, with an advance large enough to fully commit and give this full-time author career a real shot.

But all along the way, that little voice in my head kept calling me a fraud, an imposter. What business did I have writing about people having sex when I had no firsthand knowledge myself?

Sure, there was the copious amounts of smut I had read by that point, the porn I had watched, the self exploration I had done. And nothing annoyed me more than the infantilizing way society liked to treat adults who had never had sex, like it was some mile marker of adulthood. But still, that little voice in my head had persisted. *You're an imposter.*

And then, The Review.

I made it a point not to ever seek out reviews. I knew that was just asking for a mental breakdown. Reviews were for readers, and I didn't need to know all the negative things people felt about my writing. Not every book was for every person, and I knew there were people out there who *did* enjoy my writing, so that was good enough for me.

But every now and then, a review would slip through the cracks and I'd see them. You can't avoid random reviews coming across your feed as a chronically online twenty something, and you definitely can't avoid those awful posts when the reader tags you in their negative rant, forcing you to see their list of all the ways your writing was cringy and unbelievable to them. Or that your fat characters just needed to lose weight. That one was always the most annoying.

What you could never protect yourself from, however, was a famous BookTokker putting out a video that goes viral. A video where they absolutely shred your book apart and go on and on about how terrible the sex scenes were. Not just cringy and unrealistic, but written like someone who has never had sex.

Well, you got me there.

My worst nightmare had come true, but I was too chickenshit to do anything about it—not that there was really anything I could do about it directly. The Review happened not long after my second book was released last fall, and all I did was try to forget about it and retreat into my shell. I posted the bare minimum I needed to keep my social media accounts afloat, and nothing more.

I should have probably talked to a therapist about it, but I never seemed to get around to it. I hadn't spoken to one since I first got diagnosed with ADHD around 21 and tried meds. Unfortunately, the first try hadn't worked and I'd felt defeated, so I gave up instead of continuing to try like I knew I should have. I also accidentally ghosted the therapist and was too embarrassed to try to go back, so I just... never did.

And now here we were. I had been outed as the imposter I was, and I couldn't even write my next book. And if I couldn't write my next book, my career was over before it had even really started.

I closed my eyes, breathing in and out in four-second intervals, using the only calming technique I had gotten from my therapist that actually took. Four seconds, in and out, over and over until the tornado of thoughts in my head slowed to a normal speed. Well, normal for me. It was still probably a little chaotic up there to anyone who didn't have the same brain.

Getting up, I briefly glanced at myself in the full-length mirrored, sliding closet doors. I took in the dark circles under my eyes, my sallow skin, the greasy knotted hair thrown into a haphazard bun on the top of my head. At least with my black hair it wasn't as easy to notice just how greasy it was and how bad I needed to take a shower.

Not like that mattered here. My roommates wouldn't even notice. My gaze dropped down to my chest, and I remembered I wasn't wearing a bra. I threw on my comfiest sports bra before walking out into the common area.

Will, Collins, and James all sat on the couch, yelling at whatever was on the TV, beers in hand. I glanced over to see what it was and laughed under my breath when I saw *RuPaul's Drag Race.*

Yes, I did live with three male roommates, but it wasn't the typical situation you probably imagined. Sure I lived with three men, but they were the greatest guys ever and all four people in this house were queer as fuck.

As I passed the couch in the open concept living/dining room on my way to the kitchen, Collins looked up and caught my eye, sending me a wink, his blue eyes gleaming with mirth. I responded by sticking my tongue out at him. Collins and I had hit it off the second we met, the two messes we were, and now I would say he was probably my best friend.

You might wonder how I ended up with three roommates, but you try living in Orange County. You were either rich as fuck, married to someone rich as fuck, or had roommates. You could probably guess which category I fell into. Will and I had been close friends since high school. He had transferred in as a sophomore and, as a nerd and one of the only Black kids there, had struggled to fit in. My twin Noah and I, being two of the nerdiest people at the school, bonded with him right away. After college, he needed to find a place, and I was desperate to get out of my house.

Listen, I love my family more than life but living with your parents and four siblings is not exactly the life you want to live in your early twenties. I had gone to school locally and stayed at home through all four years to save money, and was so ready to get out.

Will brought in Collins, the best friend he had met in college, and we had planned to find a place just the three of us. But then we stumbled across a perfect four-bedroom unit that we just couldn't pass up. We put up an ad to find a fourth person, and James had answered. And so our little quartet had formed, and four years later here we still were.

I grabbed a Gatorade from the fridge, not being big on alcohol—much preferring weed if I wanted a buzz—and made my way to the living room. Will and James nodded hello as I plopped onto the couch next to Collins, laying my head on his shoulder, weaving my arm through his tattoo-covered arm.

"How did your writing session go, NikNak?" Collins asked.

James had started calling me that when he first moved in and found my collection of random knickknacks, and discovered I was a magpie always searching for the shiniest things. The name had then of course been picked up by Will and Collins as well, and it had stuck.

I grunted in response, and Will glanced over with a sympathetic look. "That bad, huh?"

"I'm never going to write again. I may as well just quit now."

"You could always start selling feet pics." Collins wiggled his brows at me, light brown hair flopping into his eyes.

I gave him a punch to the arm. "Oh, thank you, how helpful."

"What? I'm serious!" He held his arms up, swerving my second punch. James and Will finally pulled their attention away from the show to see what all the commotion was.

"Don't think I won't fight you just because you're huge," I snapped back. A lascivious grin bloomed on his face, and

I used my palm to push his face away. "Oh, grow up, I was talking about you being tall and beefy, not your dick. I'm sure it's very average."

Collins wiggled his eyebrows. "Beefy, am I? I promise, the package matches the rest of the body."

Will chimed in. "What are you saying about feet pics?"

Before I could respond, Collins told him, "Oh, just that our Nikki here is going to quit writing and start selling feet pics instead."

"Ooh, OK, a career change, that could be fun." Will nodded along with a straight face, playing along with Collins. "Bet you I could make more."

"You both suck. Come on, James, back me up here!"

"Oh definitely, you would make way more money than Will." James nodded sagely, his hazel eyes barely containing his mirth, before the three of them all looked at each other and burst into laughter. I huffed in annoyance, and got up to pretend to storm off. I only got one step before Will grabbed me and pulled me back down, tucking me under his arm between him and Collins.

"Come on, Nikki. For real." His voice took on a more serious tone. "Is there something any of us can do to help you? You still haven't told us what caused this writer's block."

My face heated, and I fiddled with my rings. James chimed in, "Yeah, if you tell us what's going on, maybe we could help?"

"Uhhh…" I hedged. "It's nothing specific, this one is just escaping me right now."

I love all three of my guys, and we talk about a lot of shit. But telling them that I couldn't write because someone had called my sex scenes terrible was just way too embarrassing. They were supportive of me, and not at all weird about the fact that I wrote romance like some men could be, but they weren't on Bookstagram or BookTok, so luckily they would never see or hear about The Review. Collins sometimes read romance books, but he was expressly forbidden from reading mine. I don't think I could ever look him in the eye again if he read a sex scene I wrote.

"I stared at my computer all day, so I just need a break for right now. I'll try again tomorrow."

Will tightened the arm over my shoulder, hugging me to his side, while Collins squeezed my knee.

"We're here for you, and we have faith in you. You'll get there eventually," Collins reassured me.

James leaned around from the other side of Will and patted the top of my head. "Yeah, don't worry, kid, we'll find a way to help you."

I snorted. "I'm literally a month older than you, dumbass."

"Only in age."

I burst out laughing. "You are such an idiot."

"Maybe, but I got you laughing didn't I?" He smirked, leaning back into the couch. All three of them were absolutely ridiculous, and I wouldn't trade them for the world.

The four of us settled into the couch, commenting on the action in the sow until James stood up. "Alright, I gotta get to the bar for my shift. I'll see you weirdos tomorrow."

After he left, we watched another episode of *Drag Race*. Someone on the show made a sex joke, and Collins suddenly lit up and turned to me. "I've got it!" he exclaimed, raising a finger up.

"You've got what?"

"The idea to fix your writer's block!" I raised a brow at him in expectation, and the grin on his face turned evil, "You just need to get laid."

I laughed, shoving his shoulder. It was more of a running joke in our house, since they all knew I never had, and it never bothered me. It was all in good fun, and I knew if I ever got uncomfortable with it, they'd immediately stop when I told them to.

I outwardly dismissed his joke, but it got me thinking. Could that be the solution to everything?

If I finally had sex, I would *know*. Maybe being able to translate that experience to the page would help me to actually write a sex scene that wouldn't get shredded apart online. I'd feel like less of an imposter writing about things I didn't know.

And there wass also the fact that I *wanted* to have sex. It just... hadn't happened for me yet. There was no traumatic past or anything, but the combination of me being a fat, nerdy, awkward girl growing up and being demisexual just hadn't presented me with a lot of opportunities.

But now? The more I thought about it, the more I thought, what was the harm in trying? Well, there was a lot of harm that could fall on a woman trying to have sex with a stranger, let's be real. But I'm sure there was some way to go about it relatively safely. And at this point I was desperate and willing to try anything.

With the beginnings of a new plan in motion, I bid the guys farewell and went to my room to change and head out to the bar.

I was doing this.

3

James

A Bar Song (Tipsy) - Shaboozey

I NODDED MY HEAD in greeting at Sasha, my boss and the owner of The Sleepy Siren, as I entered the break bar five minutes before my shift started. It was only eight-ish, so the bar was still dead, only the usual drunk or two stashed away in their corners, nursing their nth drink of the day. I'd been working here for four years now, since I first moved into the apartment, and I loved my job. So much so that I had quickly made my way up to the role of Assistant Manager. A job where I got to wear what I want, drink a few sips on the job, and even flirt a little with the customers? Dream job right there.

Sometimes, when I really thought about it, I couldn't believe it had only been four years that I'd been living with my roommates. No sane person would move into an apartment with three strangers, but then again, I had never claimed to be sane. And now those three weirdos were the most important people in my life.

I grabbed my apron off the hook, slinging it around my soft waist, double-checking for my notepad and pen. I snatched a clean towel, tucking it into the apron pocket before clocking in and walking out behind the bar.

"Sup." Sasha extended her fist, and I bumped it as I looked around to see what needed to get done. "You wanna prep more garnish before the rush begins?" She nodded her head towards the bowls of lemon peels, cherries, olives, and such that lined the bar, and I saw that they were indeed dwindling.

"Who else is in tonight?" I asked as I pulled out everything I needed, getting to work peeling half the lemons and slicing the other half.

"Well I won't be here for much longer actually, just need to finish up some paperwork in the back first."

"Oh, I see, too good for the rest of us plebes, huh?"

Sasha just rolled her eyes at me. She'd never admit it out loud, but I knew she loved me.

"Remind me again why I haven't fired you yet?"

"Because then you wouldn't get to see my earth-shatteringly good looks on a regular basis anymore, and then how sad would your life be?"

"Oh no, the horror," she deadpanned. I responded by winking and blowing her a kiss, which finally got her to crack a smile. "It would definitely be quieter around here without you, that's for sure."

"What I'm hearing is 'boring.'"

This time she snapped her towel at me, hitting my shoulder, which I grabbed in exaggerated pain while shouting about workers' comp.

Sasha continued as if she hadn't gotten sidetracked, "But it's going to be Peter and Megan with you tonight."

I groaned. "Why do you keep scheduling me with Megan? I keep telling you I can't stand her."

"And I keep telling you, as my assistant manager, too fucking bad."

"Why can't we fire *her*?"

Sasha closed her eyes, pinching the bridge of her nose as she took a deep breath, before turning around and ignoring me. "What! She always gets in my way and makes my drinks instead of doing her own fucking job."

"Then fucking tell her to stop!"

"You think I haven't?"

Sasha just shook her head, patting my shoulder as she walked past me to the back offices. "I'm sure you'll figure something out. You're a big boy." A smirk made its way across my face, but as I opened my mouth to respond, she threw over her shoulder, "Don't even think about it."

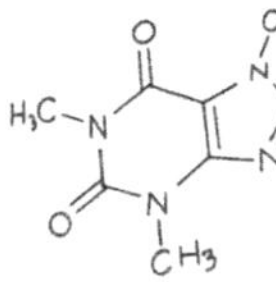

"MEGAN, GO SERVE THE other side of the bar, I got this," I spoke through gritted teeth, trying not to let my annoyance show to the customers sitting at the bar in front of us. It was ten p.m. and the height of our nighttime rush, and if she got in my space one more time I was gonna lose my damn mind.

She huffed at me, but finally went to the other side of the bar to help the customers who had been trying to get her attention. I finished up the martini I had been working on, adding the garnish before throwing the towel over my shoulder and sliding it across the counter towards the customer waiting.

She winked at me as she picked it up, swinging her hips as she walked back towards the table where a gaggle of her friends waited, watching the whole thing and bursting into whispers and giggles the second she rejoined them. I kept the pleasantly neutral look on my face, knowing that the less grumpy I looked, the more tips I would get.

But god, it was nights like this that made me question my decision to work with people for a living. I kept for-getting how much I disliked the general public. Well, more accurately that I have very little patience for stupidity, and people were very stupid. But it wasn't like there was much further Sasha could promote me here, and I really didn't want to try starting over somewhere else.

Besides, I didn't like the feelings of financial insecurity that came from leaving a job and starting a new one. Growing up with just me and my mom, I had experienced enough financial insecurity for a lifetime. It was just easier to stay the course.

The night continued on in the same way as it did every night. New customer, light flirting, rinse, repeat. I didn't want to admit it, but I felt like I was starting to fall into a rut. I was stuck, and I couldn't figure out what I wanted to do about it, what I wanted to change.

This boredom around work was affecting other parts of my life, too. As a demisexual person, I didn't often feel attracted to the person I was hooking up with—I just enjoyed sex for the act itself. But even that was beginning to lose its luster.

I felt... unmoored.

The next customer walked up, and I looked him over while I prepared his drink and handed it over to him. He was definitely the kind of person I would normally flirt with to see if my interest was reciprocated. He was tall and thin, wearing a cropped T-shirt and skinny jeans. He made eye contact with me as he brought the cup up to his face before wrapping his lips around the straw and sucking the liquid up, all while maintaining eye contact.

Alright then, definitely interested. I continued to wipe the counter, making sure he could see the grin on my face even as I looked away. But then out of the corner of my eye, I caught a flash of black hair and a body full of curves. I looked up to the other side of the bar, but the crowd had shifted and I couldn't see the person. I shook my head and went back to what I was doing. Nikki wasn't here; she was at home with Will and Collins. I needed to focus on work, not my roommate.

Maybe I should hook up with someone tonight. How long had it been? It was never a good sign when you couldn't even remember the last time you'd had sex... or who you had it with.

But that was my problem, wasn't it? I didn't care about the people I was hooking up with, I just wanted the release. I could get that by myself, sure. But it was nice to have the human contact, even when I wasn't attracted to that person. And I'd only had one sexual partner I had actually felt attracted to, and that was back in college with a long-term boyfriend. We'd been friends all through freshman and sophomore year, and I had begun to worry I was falling for him and he didn't feel the same.

That was until one night at a party after a few beers, he kissed me. And in traditional queer fashion, we moved in together a month later and stayed together for two years. We had parted amicably, but he was the one to end it, saying he felt held back by my complacency, that I never went after what I wanted. But when we were together, it had been a feeling unlike anything else.

Maybe that's what my problem was. I craved that feeling again, even more than the pleasure of sex itself. Not that it mattered, as I had no one in my life I felt that way about.

A flash of dark hair caught my eye again, and I looked up. The dark hair was gone, but the man at the counter was still devouring me with his eyes.

Fuck it, what could one more casual hookup hurt?

4

NIKKI

THIS WAS A TERRIBLE idea. Why did I think listening to *Collins* of all people was a good call? Oh, that's right, because I was sick of feeling like an impostor. Sick of wondering what it really felt like, instead of just imagining it.

So here I was, freshly showered, natural waves behaving for once, make-up on and wearing my favorite going-out dress. You know that lemon milk maid dress that everyone and their mother seemed to own if you looked at social media? Yeah, the ads got me on that one, but for once it actually turned out well.

I took a sip of my drink and looked around the crowded bar around me. I debated going somewhere new, but in the end I opted for the comfort of The Sleepy Siren instead. I figure if I was trying to do something that terrified me, I should at least be in a place that felt safe. I hadn't said hi to James yet, as he was too busy tending bar on the opposite side of the room.

Leaning back on the wall, I took a sip from my vodka apple juice I'd gotten from the other bartender on shift. The bar was a big U-shape leading from the back wall into the middle of the space. On my side, there were a few pool tables, a dart board further down the wall I was leaning on, and a long shuffleboard. On the other side of the bar, booths lined the wall while high tables were scattered the rest of the area.

The Sleepy Siren was packed tonight, all the tables and booths full, the bar itself almost completely hidden behind the people sitting or standing and waiting for their drinks. No one had paid me any mind, and I questioned whether this was a good idea or not. Did I really think I could just decide to go to a bar and get laid for the first time ever? As if I was suddenly going to stop being socially awkward around strangers and just hit up a random person.

It had been forty-five minutes now and I was just about ready to call it quits, my people-observing adventure enough excitement for one night. I pushed off the wall, slurping up the last dregs of my drink. Right as I went to set my glass down, someone bumped into me from behind.

I stumbled forward, an *oof* escaping me as my stomach slammed into the edge of the bar.

Warm hands wrapped around my waist. "Whoa there."

Shrugging out of their grip, I turned around ready to tell them off only to pull up short. The woman standing behind me was tall, with long golden-brown hair tumbling pin-straight over her light brown shoulders. The words dried up on my tongue as I took in her sparkling green eyes, which were currently looking me up and down.

The thing so many people didn't realize about attraction was that there were different kinds. Romantic, sexual, aesthetic. Demisexual people may not experience sexual attraction without an emotional connection, but we sure as hell understood aesthetic attraction. And this woman was absolutely stunning. And if I wasn't wrong, she was totally checking me out.

"How in the world did I miss *you?*" she murmured, biting her lip.

I had a choice here. Flirt back with the Amazonian goddess, or head home alone like I had planned.

"Can I buy you a drink?" The words were out of my mouth before I even decided. Well, I guess my brain decided for me. Or was it my vagina? For me, it was the idea of the act itself that tripped me up more than who my partner would be. Although, imagining her... I could feel my face beginning to heat up, and quickly tore my eyes away from hers.

I wasn't even sure if she was actually interested. I needed to get a hold of myself.

"Only if I can buy you one, too." My eyes whipped back
up to hers as a small smile grew on her mouth.

"I think I would be OK with that." We both turned back
to the bar, shoulders brushing as I flagged down James's
coworker, Megan. *I'm sure he'd be thrilled about that.* The
thought flitted across my mind, and I had to bite my lip
to keep from laughing. Wait, why was I thinking about
James? *Get your head in the game, Nikki.*

As Megan made our drinks, I turned to the woman. "So,
what's your name?" I asked, realizing that neither of us
had even bothered to ask.

She chuckled self-deprecatingly. " I guess we should
have started with that, huh?"

"Hey, we got there eventually." We both laughed, and she
tucked a chunk of hair behind her ear, before looking down
to me.

"Penny. Yours?"

"Nikki."

"Nikki." She said my name slowly, her eyes heating.
"And what are you doing at a bar all alone Nikki?"

I raised a brow at her. "Are you not also alone?"

Penny threw a look over her shoulder to a group of
women standing around one of the high tables, throwing
covert looks at us. "I am not."

"How do you know *I'm* alone then?"

"It was more hoping than knowing, if I'm being honest." Penny bit her lips, eyes dropping to my mouth as she spoke. OK, I knew I was inexperienced, but even I could tell she was laying it on *thick*. It couldn't actually be this easy, could it?

I paused for a minute, thinking about how I wanted to play this. I was just looking for a hookup, not a relationship. From the way Penny was acting, she probably also was looking just to hook up. So what was the harm in being honest, then?

"Well," I started, before taking another sip, "I am definitely here alone. What are you going to do about it?" I forced myself to keep looking her in the eye as I spoke, even a every fiber of my being rebelled against it.

Penny set her full drink down, reaching a hand out to run a finger along my cheek, watching the motion of her finger as it went. "What do you want me to do about it?" I licked my lips, setting my drink half full down on the counter and leaning into her.

"I want you to do *me.*"

I tried to school my face as my brain caught up with my mouth. Had I actually just said that? Out loud?

Well, it was out there now, and there was no taking it back. Besides, this is what I came here to do anyway. I needed to fully commit to this plan, and Penny was just as good an option as anyone.

I clenched my shaking fists, trying not to let my nerves get the best of me and bolt for the door. Penny let her hand drop to my upper arm, slowly dragging it down to my hand, until she held it in hers. She turned, aiming towards the bathroom and pulling me along behind her.

Oh my god. OK. This is really happening. I felt dizzy with anticipation, trembling with an equal mix of terror and excitement. Was this really about to happen? Just like that? Is this how allosexual people do it? Just jump right in?

Opening the door to the women's restroom, Penny threw a smirk over her shoulder, and held a finger up to her lips. As soon as I was past the door, she pushed me up against it, turning the lock and then resting her hand on my waist, the other cupping my cheek.

"God, you're so pretty," she whispered, breath fanning across my lips. As she leaned in slowly, the grip on my waist tightened, and the hand at my face slipped around to the back of my neck. I closed my eyes, tilting my chin up to meet her halfway, reaching my own hand up to grip her wrist.

My heart had either stopped beating or was beating so fast I could no longer feel it by the time her lips met mine. They were soft and warm and wet and... and I felt absolutely nothing. She tilted her hand, angling her head to kiss me deeper. It wasn't *bad,* but it did absolutely nothing for me.

I shook myself mentally, reminding my brain that I *knew* I wasn't going to feel a spark or butterflies. That didn't mean I couldn't enjoy the act itself, right? I kissed her back, trying to ignore the buzzing of the lights above us, the sour smell of a bar bathroom, the way my shoes were sticking to the floor.

She brushed her tongue along the seam of my lips, seeking entrance, and I opened myself up to her. That was when things really started going downhill. The feeling of her tongue in my mouth was... weird. Weird and so, so wet. The strange feeling of her tongue plunging into my mouth was all I could focus on, and I couldn't enjoy myself of the kiss.

Finally, she broke away, gasping for air. Her hand gave my waist a squeeze, before slowly drifting down my thigh to toy with the hem of my dress. "How do you want me?" Penny kissed along my neck lightly, the feeling more ticklish than sensual. I closed my eyes, trying to picture it. Grinding against her thigh, or riding her hand, or her kneeling on this disgusting-ass floor to eat me out? None of those options sounded appealing or sexy in any way.

Decision made, I braced myself for her reaction. "I'm so sorry, I don't think I can do this." My breaths were starting to come fast, the edges of panic closing in on me.

Penny's fingers gently tilted my chin up to look at her. "Hey, are you OK?'

I gulped before responding, "I'm OK, I swear. I'm so sorry, I really thought I could do this, but I just can't." My voice picked up pitch and speed as I continued to babble, "You see, I'm demi and I don't normally do this and I just—"

"Hey," she said softly. "It's OK.'

"Really? You're not mad?" The words came out of me a whisper.

"No." She laughed softly, only the barest hint of disappointment in her eyes. "You don't owe me anything, not even an explanation."

I felt every muscle in my body loosen at her words, not even realizing just how tense I had gotten the longer we kissed. "Thank you," I muttered weakly. She gave me one last smile before I turned and unlocked the door, swinging it open and bolting for the door. I wanted to fall into a very deep, very dark pit and never come back out.

5

James

BUILD ME UP BUTTERCUP - THE FOUNDATIONS

"...FATHER, PREPARE TO DIE!"

I paused right inside the doorway, just out of view of the couch, and cursed under my breath. Coming home to find *The Princess Bride* playing was *never* a good sign.

Locking the door behind me, I dropped my keys in the bowl on the stand by the door, taking a moment to collect myself before going to find her. It had been a long night, and I had decided against a casual hookup with the hot guy who had been eye-fucking me. I was trying and failing to convince myself that it wasn't because I thought I saw

Nikki for the third time, running out the front door of the bar this time.

I made my way to the living room and sure enough, there was Nikki, fluffy blanket wrapped around her shoulders and head like a little turtle, bowl of ice cream in hand, staring dejectedly at the TV. I hated seeing her upset. Because I hated seeing any of my friends upset, of course—not just her specifically.

"What's up, buttercup? I wasn't expecting you to still be up." I flopped onto the couch next to her, throwing my feet up on the coffee table. She glared at me, looking between my face and the shoes on the table. I rolled my eyes, kicking them off onto the floor. "Better, your majesty?"

"Please, you menace, we don't have to be royals to not put shoes on a coffee table."

I ignored her valid point and instead nodded at the TV, raising my brow in question. Curiously, her cheeks flamed red, and she sunk deeper into the blanket.

"Oooh, juicy drama! Tell me!" I rested my chin on folded hands, fluttering my lashes at her. Nikki tried to fight the smile forming on her lips, and I tried to ignore the way my chest warmed in approval at getting a positive reaction from her.

"Be quiet, I'm trying to watch my movie." She shushed me before turning back to the screen and pretending to watch. She definitely didn't need to watch; she could probably quote the entire thing from memory. I reached over her to grab the remote, my elbow accidentally brushing her breasts as I went. I quickly leaned back into the couch and paused the movie, hoping my face didn't show a blush. I turned to her expectantly.

Nikki huffed in exasperation. "OK, you just have to promise you won't laugh at me." She set her ice cream bowl on the table.

I gasped in mock outrage, a hand to my chest. "*Laugh* at you? I would never!" She stared, unamused at my antics. "Besides, of course, all the times I have laughed at you before. And probably will again if we're being perfectly hone—" My words were cut off when she hit me in the face with one of the couch pillows. "Fair enough, please continue."

She looked down at her hands instead of speaking. I sat quietly and waited, knowing she would start speaking when she was ready.

"I tried to hook up with someone tonight." She looked at me tentatively, like she was searching for reproach or judgement. Why she thought I, of all people, would judge her was so beyond me it hurt my feelings a little bit. But all I did was nod in encouragement for her to continue, ignoring the twinge I felt at the thought of her hooking up with someone. Wait, no, I felt no twinge. There was no twinge because there were no feelings because she was my *friend* and that was it.

"It, uh, didn't go well."

"What a relief. I would hate to see how you reacted if this is what you looked like after a *good* experience."

She glared at me. "Jackass," she mumbled under her breath before continuing. "I came by The Sleepy Siren after Collins and Will convinced me I should try hooking up with someone to get me out of my slump."

So I *had* seen her tonight at the bar. It made me feel slightly better that I wasn't seeing her in places she wasn't. I tried ignoring the way that made me feel, and tried to focus on Nikki's feelings instead of my own.

"Why in the world would you take advice from them?"

"I know." She grinned wryly. "I definitely learned my lesson there."

"For real, though, why would they suggest you try a hook up and why would you actually do it?"

She stiffened. "Why is me hooking up with someone so wild of an idea?"

"No, no, no, that's not what I meant." I pinched the bridge of my nose, trying to gather my thoughts and not put my foot in my mouth again. "I meant why would hooking up with someone help with your writer's block, and why would you go do something you don't really seem to want to do?"

A deep sigh gusted out of her, and she seemed to deflate. She picked at the skin around her nails rather than look-ing back at me. She mumbled something under her breath I couldn't hear.

"What?" I ducked down, trying to get closer to hear.

"I said, I need to have sex so I can write!"

I blinked in confusion.

"You all know I've never had sex, but you don't know that my writer's block is because I got called out in a viral review on social media for having 'unrealistic sex scenes' written by 'someone who seems like they've never actually had sex.'" She used air quotes as she spoke, voice cloaked in frustration.

I choked on my own breath as I took in her words. "I see..."

"I told you not to laugh at me!"

I raised my hands in defense. "I'm not laughing!" But I was biting my lip to hold back the grin trying to break out across my face.

"I will throw another pillow at your face, I swear to Princess Buttercup."

At that I did finally break down laughing, and it only took a moment for her to join me. "So they all found out the big secret, huh?"

"It's not like I was out there lying saying I'm some sex-pert or something! Sometimes being a romance author is so weird. In what other job, besides sex work of course, do people question you about your sex life? With sex work-ers, their life is their work, so I know it's a little differ-ent, and of course writing smutty romance or erotica has crossover with sex work, but that's a whole other discus-sion. But man, sometimes readers have so little respect for authors as people. The amount of invasive questions romance authors get about their sex lives is so gross. If it's not offered freely, it's none of your damn business!"

"Damn, seriously? That's so messed up."

"It really is! Just because I write about people having sex doesn't mean strangers get to ask me about my personal sex life."

"So, about that sex life..."

Nikki rolled her eyes. "Collins made the same joke he always does about me just needing to get laid, and this time, I actually thought about it and it made sense. When I write about something I don't have actual experience with, I research it. So this was like, I dunno, research? I just thought, maybe if I finally have sex it will make me feel like less of an imposter."

"Well you make research sound a lot more fun than I remember it being in college." A laugh barked out of her at that, and I preened to myself that I had managed to cheer her up. "So what happened? Are you a bad kisser?" I pretended like my heart didn't beat just a little faster at the idea of kissing her.

"Why do you assume *I* was the bad kisser? Maybe I'm an amazing kisser, and she was the one who sucked." Her lips twitched at her own wording, and I snorted, trying very hard not to acknowledge the thought of just how good a kisser she might be.

"And was there? Sucking?" I asked, enjoying just how red her face got.

"We never got past the kiss. I just... I couldn't do it."

"Ah well, you gave it the old college try. What's the next idea to get you over your slump? I hear they're doing some great things in porn lately. You should try that instead."

"Psh, if you think I don't already watch porn—ethical porn, by the way, thank you very much—then you're dumber than I thought."

I cleared my throat, squirming in my spot, doing my absolute best not to picture exactly that when she was close enough to see just how tight my pants were starting to get with this line of conversation. Nikki seemed to realize what she said after saying it and clammed up, looking down to her fingers again. But I didn't miss the pink tinge to her cheeks.

"I'm gonna try again, just maybe not in a bar bathroom after five minutes this time."

"Right, of course. That makes sense."

"How do you do it?"

My eyes widened. "How do I… have sex?" I could barely get the words out, my skin suddenly feeling too tight for my body.

"Oh my god!" She buried her face in her hands. "Oh god, that's not what I meant. I just meant, you're demi, too. How do you do casual hookups?"

"Oh." My heart rate slowed back down, and I thought about it for a moment before responding. "Well, most of the time I'm still not physically attracted to the partner I hook up with. I just do it because it feels good. Like, I don't feel sparks or butterflies, but sometimes it feels good to get off by something other than my own hand." Now it was my turn to blush and avoid looking her in the eyes, but I didn't really know how else to explain it.

"You know demisexuality is a spectrum. Attraction versus action and all that. And of course there's the differences in sexual orientation versus sex drive as well. But just like most people on the asexual spectrum—or, let's be real, most human beings in general—I go through different periods of libido. Times when it's higher, times when it's not." I shrugged, trying to pretend like I was completely unaffected by this conversation. The four of us talked about a lot of stuff, but Nikki and I had never truly had in-depth conversations about sex one-on-one before. I had always made damn sure of that.

She hummed in response, staring thoughtfully at the scene paused on the screen. "I guess that makes sense. And I'm not in any rush to be in a relationship necessarily. Or like I think that I need to have a sexual experience to be valid. But I *want* to experience it. Not because I feel like it will make me a 'real adult' or any of that bullshit, but because *I* want to. It just doesn't seem like it'll ever happen to me at this point."

"Nikki, look at me." She looked up, eyes hesitant, braced for impact. "If you want it to, it will. It just needs to be with the right person for *you.*"

She shot me a small smile. "Thanks, James."

Nikki unpaused the movie, and we both settled back into the couch. I wanted to say more, but I also didn't want to push her.

Because in the deepest recesses of my soul, part of me thought I was the right person for her.

6

James

The Green Dragon - Billy Boyd, Dominic Monaghan, & Howard Shore

Tonight had been absolute ass. Saturdays were always the busiest days of the week working at a bar, and tonight was no exception. Add to that, we were short-staffed, and my night was ruined.

The only good thing about it being so nonstop busy was that it left me very little time to think about my conversation with Nikki last night. If I was being honest with myself, it was all I had been thinking about. And I had to stop. I kept Nikki very firmly in the friend box in my mind, and she was not allowed to wander anywhere else up there.

She was my friend, and friendly feelings were the only kind I could have about her. One conversation about her sex life was not going to change that. At least, that was what I was telling myself. Because last night's feelings were a one-time thing. I was just horny. We were talking about sex, and that was that. It was nothing else.

It *couldn't* be anything else.

"Earth to James?" Sasha's voice snapped me out of my thoughts, and I realized I had been wiping the same extremely clean glass for minutes now, and Sasha was giving me her *I'm going to kill you if you don't get it together* look. "Maybe wanna do your job and help the horde of customers waiting for you to get your head out of your ass?"

"I dunno, wanna foot out first so I can get my head out?"

"What does that even mean?" she asked incredulously.

"Eh, I tried something, it didn't work." I shrugged, setting the glass and cloth down, and made my way down the bar towards her.

"You are so weird."

"Hey, I keep your life interesting. You're welcome." I turned to take an order before she could say anything else and pretended I didn't notice when she snapped the towel in her hand at my arm.

The time flew as I made drink after drink for the next few hours.

Finally getting a break in the crowd, I took advantage of the moment to wipe my station down and restock my glasses from the dishwasher. But right as I turned to the back, a wolf whistle broke out, and a man's voice called out, "Oh, who's that hottie behind the bar?"

Recognizing the voice, I made sure to shake my ass a little extra as I continued on my way rather than turning and acknowledging him.

A trio of cackles broke out behind me, and I let a grin spread across my face. In the madness, I had totally forgotten they were going to come entertain me tonight. I made my way back out with a clean rack of glasses, dropping them on the counter and turning to my three waiting friends. Will, Collins, and Nikki sat left to right on the bar stools, elbows on the bar, chins resting on their clasped hands, fluttering their lashes at me in unison.

"Free drinks, please!" they chorused out as one.

"Menaces, the lot of you," I shot back at them, but the laughter in my voice definitely undermined the name calling. I attempted, in vain, to keep my eyes from lingering too long on NIkki and the soft curves and rolls of her body under the crop top and maxi skirt she wore. The soft, loose curls of her black hair falling around her shoulders. The clear blue eyes twinkling in mischief along with the two idiots beside her.

"So how's it been tonight?" Collins asked as he glanced around at the mostly packed bar. "Looks pretty busy in here."

"Let's just say we had a callout which made it worse, but it was Megan, so it's also better," I replied dryly. They all cringed in unison. They had heard many a complaint about Megan in our venting sessions—or as we liked to call them, roommate trauma-bonding sessions.

"Two nights in a row, and you might have killed her," Collins quipped.

"Might?" I started pulling glasses out. "The usuals?"

"You treat us so well." Will sighed dreamily at me, and I blew him a kiss. He pretended to swoon, falling into Collins's shoulder.

As I made their drinks, I snuck glances at Nikki who was very much *not looking at me*. Maybe she was just as affected by our conversation last night as I was. As I made a Cosmo for Will, a lemon drop for Collins, and a vodka apple juice for Nikki, the three of them picked up where they must have left off in their conversation on their way here.

"I'm telling you, it's an allegory for *Macbeth*," Will insisted, while Collins shook his head vehemently.

"What is?" I set their glasses on the bar in front of me, wiping my hands off on the towel thrown over my shoulder.

"That scene from the last *Lord of the Rings*! Eowyn's big moment."

"And I'm just saying I don't see it." Collins threw up his arms in surrender, and Will made a sound of distress like he was actually being tortured, rather than dealing with our idiot roommate who also had a not-so-secret love of riling him up. I decided to take pity on him this time.

"Tell me, how so?" My eyes flicked over to Nikki only to see she was already looking at me, a small, fond smile on her face as she shook her head at their antics.

"OK, so you know how Eowyn is able to kill the Witch-King because no man can kill him, but she's a woman, right?"

"Alright, I'm with you."

"Well, he's paying homage to *Macbeth* with that line, obviously! In *Macbeth*, it's the *witches* who tell Macbeth '*None of woman born shall harm Macbeth.*' But then later you find out Macduff was delivered by C-section, so on a technicality, he was not woman born, yeah?"

"OK." Collins nodded along slowly, stroking his chin like a cartoon villain pretending to think, but Will was too far gone on his tangent to notice, staring at me instead. Out of the corner of my eye I could see Nikki stifling a giggle into her glass.

Will made the universal duh gesture, and when Collins didn't immediately respond, Will finally looked over and saw what Collins was doing. He lifted a finger, pointing it accusingly at Collins and grumbling about impossible people, while the three of us burst into laughter.

Just when it looked like he was about to explode, Collins finally gave in, speaking through his laughter, hands aloft placatingly. "OK, OK, I'm sorry! Of course I know 'no man' is a reference to no 'man woman born,' I was just messing with you."

Will just shook his head, *tsking* at Collins. "Man, sometimes I really can't with you."

"Then don't make it so damn easy." Collins grinned, slinging his arm over Will's shoulders. As they devolved into a scuffle, I leaned on the bar in front of Nikki, forearms resting on the edge, rocking on the balls of my feet towards her. When I looked up to meet her eyes, a shot of electricity zoomed through me.

Nikki

THE VEINS ON JAMES'S arms bulged as he pressed his forearms further into the edge of the bar, and my eyes traced along the black lines of the tattoo on the inside of his right forearm. It was the molecular breakdown of caffeine, in honor of his coffee addition. Our shared love of that magical bean was the first thing we bonded over.

James nodded his head towards Dumb and Dumber, leaning in to murmur, "How long have they been at this?"

I take in his profile. The dusting of reddish-tinged dark brown scruff. Hair reaching his ears, wave pattern just barely discernable. Hazel eyes glinting jovially behind his wire-framed glasses.

His jawline hid behind the soft roundness of his face, the slightly rounded belly of his "dad bod" pressing where his shirt was tucked into his jeans under his open flannel. And his nails were painted—currently a dark enough blue that they almost looked black—only slightly beginning to chip at the edges.

I had never really paid much attention to his physical appearance, never noticed the space he took up or the way he moved. But ever since our conversation last night, I couldn't *stop* thinking about it. James cleared his throat, and I remembered he just asked me a question. I hoped he couldn't see the blush I felt staining my cheeks.

"Oh, you know, just for the past hour or so." James shook his head, pushing back from the counter, and I tried not to shiver at the loss of warmth in my space. I looked over to Will and Collins instead, who had finally finished their fight and were now tearing up over what looked to be a cute animal video on Collins's phone.

I took a sip of my drink, watching as James made his way down the bar taking people's orders. My eyes caught on the way the muscles in his forearms shifted as he shook a drink, the sleeves of his flannel pushed up to his elbows. The way his smile was just a little crooked as he smiled at a flirty customer, leaning into the bar the way he had done just a minute ago with me. I watched as he winked at them, a blush rising in their cheeks as they looked up at James through their lashes.

I wish it came as easily to me as it seemed to James. He was so naturally flirty, the turn of his lips making you feel like you were constantly in on some inside joke with him. He would never have a problem finding someone to hook up with. He never seemed to have a problem in the past, that's for sure.

My mind wandered back to last night and our conversation again. I had never talked with him so openly about sex before. There was definitely a difference in making sex jokes with your friends versus actually *talking* about your sex lives, and last night was definitely the latter.

As uncomfortable as I had been in the moment, as I was anytime I tried discussing my sex life with people, it had actually helped a lot. It made me realize that if I really was going to actively seek out my first sexual experience, it had to be with someone I trusted. And definitely someone who knew what they were doing.

It almost made me think... but no. I shook my head, trying to unthink that thought. Because if I went down that road, there was no coming back. And just because he was able to easily flirt and hook up with strangers did not mean he would be open to... what? What did I even think I would ask him? To *teach* me how to have sex? How absolutely ridiculous. I forced myself to look away from James and join in on Will and Collins's conversation.

7

NIKKI

WE'RE FUCKED, IT'S FINE - JEREMY ZUCKER

"I THINK I'M LOSING my mind." I was laid out on the floor of my room, staring at the ceiling and contemplating all my life choices.

"Why are you always so dramatic?" My twin sister's voice drifted back to me over the speaker of my phone where it lay on the floor next to my head.

"Rude, I'm not *dramatic.* I'm being perfectly reasonable in this assessment."

"And why do you say that?"

"Because I'm thinking about asking James to have sex with me?"

There was a brief moment of complete silence before Noah responded.

"I'm on my way."

Oh fuck, I really was losing my mind if she was facing SoCal morning traffic to drive to me instead of just talking on the phone. "So this is an insane idea, then?"

I heard the sounds of keys jangling, a door closing, and the rev of the engine as she started her car, a moment passing before the sound swapped over to the car system. "First, we don't use that word anymore, because we do not perpetuate harmful stereotypes about mental health struggles. Second, can I ask *why* you want to ask James to have sex with you?"

"Sorry," I murmured, properly chastened. Noah was a pediatrician and cared deeply about not only physical health, but mental health. She also was autistic, and language was a special interest of hers, so she was always on top of words that people were trying to change the use of. It was jarring to realize just how many words we used in today's vocabulary that had horribly racist or ableist origins. I could always count on her to remind me when I forgot and slipped into an old habit.

"So this is a ridiculous idea?"

"Better." I could picture her decisive nod of approval in my mind and couldn't help but smile at the image. "Now answer my second question," she demanded.

"Because of the bad review?" I nervously chewed my lip while I waited for her response.

"I'm gonna need a little more context than that, babe."

A deep sigh gusted me as I sat up, turning to lean my back against the foot of my bed. Drawing my legs up I rested my chin on my knees, arms wrapped around my bent legs. "You know I haven't been able to write since that review went viral?" She hummed in the affirmative, so I kept going. "Well, the other night Collins made the joke again that I should just get laid and it got me thinking."

"That you should solicit one of your friends for sex? One of your friends who you happen to *live with,* might I remind you?"

"Hey, I told you I was losing my mind! You should have taken me seriously!"

"Alright, alright. Keep talking. How did you get from 'need to get laid' to James?"

"Wellllll…" I dragged the word out, picking at a loose string unraveling from the hem of my shorts.

"Nikki Alexandra Stone." None of us Stone siblings had middle names, so Noah took it upon herself, as the oldest sibling, to assign random middle names whenever she was trying to use her mom voice on us. Mind you, we were twins and she was all of five minutes older than me, and also not actually a mom. Though if you tried telling her that having her cat did not make her a mother, you would *never* hear the end of it.

I buried my face in my hands, mumbling into them.

"What was that?" I heard the telltale signs of a car parking and the sound switched back over to her phone. Her heels clicked on the sidewalk as she walked up to my front door.

"I tried to hook up with a stranger from The Sleepy Siren two days ago." Her footsteps stopped. "It didn't go great." My phone beeped, and I looked down to see the call had ended. A moment later my door banged open, and Noah strode in. Although we were fraternal, we still looked very similar. The same plus-size body, the same blue eyes, the same loose black curls—though she kept hers dip-dyed on the ends in a rotation of bright colors. At the moment it was a bright emerald green.

"Bitch, I can't believe you finally tried to have sex and didn't tell me first!" Noah flopped down on the floor next to me and reached over to tug on a lock of my hair. I swatted her hand away.

"Ugh, I know. It just all happened so fast, and I know you're busy at work right now." I looked down, picking at the skin around my nails, until Noah covered my hands with her own to stop me.

"I am never too busy for you. When will you get that through that thick skull of yours?"

I groaned, letting my head fall back on the bed behind me as I stared at the ceiling, avoiding looking at my sister. She was the one person I could never truly hide what I was feeling from. I didn't respond right away, and Noah didn't push me, just let me get there on my own. We sat in silence just for a few moments longer as I gathered my thoughts.

"To be fair, I didn't tell *anyone*." She opened her mouth, and I continued before she could jump in. "And yes, I am well aware that you're not just anyone. It's just, this is one of the few things that you will never fully be able to understand because you're not demi. You don't experience attraction the same way, and you don't deal with the in-fantilization I face as a virgin in her mid-twenties."

"You're right," Noah agreed. "I'll never fully be able to understand, but I *will* always be here for you."

"I know." I slung my arm over her shoulders, resting my head on hers. "And I love you for that. But this time, I just wanted to do it on my own. I didn't know what was going to happen, and I didn't really want to talk about it in the moment."

"OK, so walk me through everything that happened."

And so, I told her everything. How much more I had been struggling with my writer's block since The Review, more than I had let on. My call with Lucy and their quip about buying a new vibrator. Collins's joke about me needing to get laid and how it made me think. Going to the bar and being about to bail when I met Poppy.

"She was so pretty, Noah, I swear. I have no idea what she was doing talking to me."

Noah gasped. "Rude!" I leveled her with a look, but she persisted. "Don't insult my looks like that."

I rolled my eyes. "We started talking, and she was laying it on thick, and I thought it was going to be so easy just getting right at it." I covered my hands in embarrassment. "So we went to the bathroom and she kissed me against the door and I feel like it *should* have been super hot but it just… wasn't. I couldn't get out of my head, and all I could think was how weird it was that this random stranger had her tongue in my mouth." I still can't believe I did that.

"Damn, girl, five minutes and right to the bathroom? No wonder it didn't go well! That's fast even for allo people."

"Ugh, I know, it was, wasn't it?"

"Alright, so I'm with you all the way through the failed hookup, but where does James come in? You've never been interested in him before, so why now?"

"I wouldn't go so far as to say I'm *interested* in him." My face twisted in concentration, trying to put to words what I was feeling and thinking. "It's more that he feels *safe*. You know he's demi, too, but also is kind of a manwhore?" She raised her brow at that statement, but didn't interrupt. "Well, that night when he got home from work he found me on the couch watching *The Princess Bride*, and we actually had kind of a long conversation about sex." I could feel the blush rising on my cheeks but chose to ignore it, and prayed Noah wouldn't tease me for it.

"I caved and told him what caused my writer's block, and about my ridiculous idea of finding someone random. He didn't judge me, just listened. And when I got up the courage to ask him how it was so easy for him to hook up with people as a demi, he actually took the time to think about it and give me a real answer, not that he owed me anything. It got me thinking... well, you know. He's got plenty of experience, he's someone safe I know and trust, and he understands a part of me that no one else in my life does."

Noah reached over, squeezing my hand in comfort, and I sighed before continuing. "I know it doesn't seem like a good idea, but then last night Will, Collins, and I all went to hang out at the bar while James was working, and watching the way he was with customers... everything just comes so *easily* to him. I have no doubt he'd be able to help me learn about fucking! Have you seen him at the bar? Those hands *definitely* know what they're doing."

"Nikki, love of my life, mate of my soul, twin of my womb, you are absolutely bonkers."

I burst out laughing, but Noah just continued shaking her head at me as she had been. "Listen, I actually am on board with this whole"—she waved her hand over my body as she spoke—"'Nikki gets out there and finally gets some' thing. Not because you *have* to, but because you want to. But is asking James really a good idea?"

"You really think it would be that bad?" I chewed on my lip, every way in which this idea could blow up in my face running through my head.

"I've seen that man at work. I don't think bad is in his vocabulary when it comes to sex." She smirked at me, and I shoved her until she tipped over onto the floor in retaliation. "Just kidding. You know I would never touch one of your roommates. That's just asking for something messy to happen, and you know I don't do messy." It was true, she didn't—a least, not usually. "But anyways, no. I didn't mean I think the sex would be bad. I mean, are you sure this won't ruin your friendship?"

"Honestly?" I straighten up, pushing my shoulders back and speaking with a confidence I don't yet actually feel. "I know there's a chance it could. But James has almost exclusively casual sex, so why is it so wild to think he could have casual sex with me? Besides, I can't think of anyone else I could trust to teach me, and obviously it's not going to work with a stranger, so what option do I have?"

She sighed. "So many other options, Nikki. So many. Many that don't involve having sex with your friend-slash-roommate."

"I have to get this book written, Noah! It is so past due, there's no way they'll give me another extension. I'm still waiting to hear back from Lucy about what they're going to say about asking for *this* extension. Lucy is so patient with me, but I can't keep doing this to them. And if what I need to fix my sex scenes is research, then research it is."

"God, that sentence is so weird."

I cracked a smile. "I know right? This really is equal parts the best and worst job, isn't it?"

"So." She smirked. "You're going to do *him* for the plot?"

"Literally," I shot back as we both dissolved into laughter. I didn't get that much time with Noah anymore, so

these were the moments I really treasured, just being together. But she had a life to get back to, and eventually she
had to get going.

Noah heaved a deep sigh as she stood up, reaching an
arm down to help me do the same. "Well, I may not like
this plan, but it seems as if you have actually thought it
out. Though, as a romance author, you should know that
the casual sex trope only ever ends in one of two ways."

I waved off her concerns as I walked her to the front
door and hugged her goodbye. "Please. Like you said. I'm a
romance author. I totally know what I'm doing."

8

NIKKI

BAD DECISIONS - THE STROKES

I HAD NO IDEA what the fuck I was doing. I was pacing a hole in the carpet in front of my closet, staring at the clothes inside, wondering which of my outfits said "Hey, roomie! Wanna teach me how to have sex so I can write my romance book and pay the rent so I don't have to move out or become homeless?"

Little black dress was probably too sexy, but comfy at-home clothes were far too casual. Maybe jeans? *Ugh,* no. I dropped to the edge of my bed, running my hands up and through my hair so I could grip it and tug lightly. It was one of the ways I stimmed for self-soothing. The pressure and very slight sting felt more comforting than painful, and gave my brain something to focus on other than my spiraling thoughts.

It had been two hours since Noah left, and I had spent that entire time freaking out over what outfit to wear when I asked James. *Worrying this much over just the outfit is not a good sign for how this is going to go, Nikki.* I told my brain to shut the fuck up.

"Well, well, well, what's going on in here?" A voice filled with amusement floated in from the open door, and I looked up to find Collins leaning against my open door frame, taking in the explosion of clothes across my room.

"I'm looking for an outfit?" The words squeaked out of me, unsure, and I cringed, my shoulders hiking up to my ears.

"Are you asking or telling me?" He raised a brow, coming farther into the room. "It looks like a hurricane went through here." He looked around, picking a lacy bra up off the bed and waggling his brows at me. I snatched it from his fingers and shoved it behind an overflowing laundry basket in the closet. Collins walked over to me, putting his hands on my shoulders until I stopped fidgeting and looked at him. It was probably all the experience he had dealing with his own ADHD, but he always knew just what to do and say when I got overstimulated.

"Breathe." He kept eye contact with me as he loudly breathed in for four seconds, hold for four, out for four, hold another four. We repeated this three times until I was finally calm enough to really see through the spiraling thoughts clogging up my brain. He was always good at helping me calm down when I needed to.

"Hit me with it. What's got you all..." He gestured at me with both of his hands in a chaotic motion.

I chewed on my lip, trying to think of what I was supposed to tell him. I had forgotten to think about Will and Collins in all of this. What would they think of it? Should I even tell them? Definitely not before asking James. What if James just laughed in my face? No, he wouldn't do that. There was a chance that he would reject me, and that was something I just had to accept if I really wanted to go through with this. But he would never laugh at me.

Telling Collins or Will was out of the question right now. Maybe James and I would just do our *research* and then never talk about it again, and no one else would ever need to know!

Sure, this was totally going to work, and not blow up in my face at all.

I'd always found the best way to get away with a little white lie was to base it in truth, "I'm trying to figure out what to wear to ask someone to hook up with me?"

Collins's brows raised all the way to his hairline, letting out a low whistle. "Damn, she's got balls."

I pushed on. "So, don't let this go to your head, but after your comment the other day-"

"You know I love you," Collins started seriously, cutting me off, and I side-eyed him, wondering where he was going with this, "but it's more of a sisterly way. I'm very flattered that you want a piece of me—"

"Oh please." I shoved his shoulder, knocking him off balance as he burst into laughter. "I would never sleep with you." I shuddered in disgust, and he gasped in mock outrage.

"*Anyways*," I said pointedly, "it just kind of made sense. Maybe to get out of my head, I need to, I don't know, get *into* my body?" I shuddered when I realized what I'd said. "Oh my god, that sounded so much worse out loud than it did in my head."

I sat down on the edge of my bed, Collins following next to me.

"I know I've asked before, but the jokes haven't been making you uncomfortable, have they?"

My heart filled with warmth at the genuine concern in his voice and in his eyes as he looked at me, and I smiled.

"I promise I would have told you if they did. But thank you for checking in about it. I promise this decision has more to do with me than with your jokes. It just got me thinking."

"OK. Good." He slung an arm over my shoulder, squeezing me to him while he rested his head on top of mine. "You know I love you like the sister I always wanted."

"I know." I snaked my arm around his back, hugging him in return. "Speaking of sisters, guess who you just missed?"

"Not possible, since she doesn't exist."

"She exists!"

"I don't believe you!" Collins shot back in a sing-song voice as he stood.

"Just because you haven't seen her yet doesn't mean she doesn't exist, you dork."

Collins had a running joke that I was making Noah up since he had never been in the same room as her. With their extremely busy schedules—he was a firefighter and she was a pediatrician—their paths had just never crossed.

"Yeah, I'll believe it when I see it."

"I have literally shown you photos of her before!"

"Um, Photoshop? Those are just pictures of yourself you've edited."

I threw a pillow at him, but he ducked out of the doorway just in time, cackling as he went. Shaking my head with a smile on my face, I looked around at the explosion of clothing on the floor. The smile slowly faded as what I was about to do tonight came back to me.

God, how was I going to do this? How would I even get James alone to ask? And then what would I do? I'd just say, *Hey, James, I know we've been friends for years and we live together and we don't want to date each other, but will you teach me how to have sex so I can get back to writing my smutty little books and then we'll move on with our lives like it never happened?*

Before I could spiral any further, my phone started ringing. I dug it out from where it was buried beneath a pile of shorts to see Lucy's name flash across my screen. Honestly, with my internal breakdown the past few days, I had forgotten I was waiting for them to call me back about the extension.

Stealing myself, I answered the call and lifted the phone to my ear, injecting my voice with forced cheer. "Hey, Lucy!"

"Nikki! I'm sure you've been waiting for my update." They got straight to business like always, and the familiarity of it all soothed some of my anxiety over what news they had for me.

"Just a little." My laugh was strained, and I gripped my phone so tight I was sure my knuckles had turned white.

"Well, I have good news for you. The publisher is willing to give you one last extension."

The breath released from me on a sigh, my entire body loosening in relief at their words. "Oh, thank god."

I could hear the smile in their voice turning serious as they continued, "Don't get too comfortable now. They're giving you this extension, but it's your *last* one. If they don't have it in their hands by December first, they're canceling the book and dropping you."

Three more months. I had three more months to figure my shit out and get this book written and turned in. I took a deep breath. I can do this. I *know* I can do this. And now, I had a plan of action.

"Nikki?" With a start, I realized I never responded, so lost in my own head with relief.

"Sorry! Yes, I'm here, just doing the mental math."

They chuckled. "Good. Did you think about what I said last time? Do you have a plan to get you out of this slump?"

I thought about James, and my face flushed as I tried to figure out what to say. "Um, yep! I have a plan I'm working on." I chewed on my lip hoping they wouldn't ask me for any further details, not knowing what in the world I would say to them if they did.

"Good! I'm proud of you." I don't know why they believed in me so much—god knows I'd done little to deserve it—but I was grateful for them nonetheless. "Now get back to it, yeah? I'll check in with you soon."

We hung up, and with a renewed sense of determination, I began going through my clothes again.

9

NIKKI

CLOSER - TEAGAN AND SARA

APPARENTLY, A PAIR OF ripped up boyfriend jeans and your favorite crop top were the best outfit to wear to ask your friend/roommate to fuck you for *research*. I got lucky with the roommate gods, because today both Will and Collins would be at work—Collins having left for a forty-eight hour shift right after our conversation, Will out covering a pre-season Rams day game at his job as a radio sportscaster.

James wasn't working until tonight, so the two of us would be home alone together all afternoon. My heart had been racing since I ended the call with Lucy, knowing that this was my one shot to broach the topic with him. But this idea could all end up being for nothing. If James wasn't comfortable with this of course I wasn't going to try and convince or coerce him.

What if he wasn't attracted to me? He'd never made any indication that he was before. Sure, he may not need to find me attractive to sleep with me, since he slept with people he wasn't attracted to somewhat often, but that felt different.

And alternatively, what if he *was* attracted to me and we had sex and it ruined our friendship?

I shook my head, forcing myself to stop spiraling about it before there was anything to spiral about. I had decided to do this, consequences be damned, so now it was time.

I took one last look at myself in the mirror that acted as my closet door and examined myself. The roundness of my stomach, and the squishy roll above the waist of the jeans. The faint stretch lines you could see on the exposed skin between the pants and the hem of my soft, formfitting red cropped t-shirt. My boobs were on the smaller side for someone of my size, my body in the shape of a pear. The textured strawberry skin of my exposed biceps. My soft double chin, the slightest scattering of freckles across the bridge of my nose and cheeks, more faint than usual since I hadn't spent much time outside since becoming a full-time author.

Man, I really needed to get out more, but it was so easy to fall into a pattern of never leaving the house when you worked from home. Even more so when you have mental health struggles. I had gone through phases of hating my body, like most people, *especially* most fat people. My relationship with my body was now the best it had ever been. I loved my softness and my strength. I found the beauty in the stretch marks and even the cellulite. I also stopped prescribing worth and value to what my body looked like.

That didn't mean I didn't still have hard days, though. I hated this mentality that often came with body positivity, that we had to love ourselves completely and indefinitely all the time, or we didn't truly love ourselves at all. But it wasn't like you couldn't wholeheartedly love a partner and still struggle with them, still have bad days. I'd recently heard the phrase "body neutrality" and it's one that I had been thinking a lot about lately. Body neutrality focused more on accepting and appreciating your body for what it was, rather than what it looked like. I was so proud of myself for getting to a place where I could look in the mirror and catalogue my body like that without feeling any type of way, just appreciating myself for exactly how I was.

My body had carried me through twenty-six years, and I loved it for that. I loved it because it was mine, and that was enough for me. I could no longer get on board with the toxic positivity of loving my body always. I was allowed to have bad days and still love and respect myself.

After another moment gazing in the mirror, I finally felt ready. Ready to put myself out there and *try*. Tilting my chin up and pushing my shoulders back, I forced myself to fake the confidence until I could feel it. What's the worst that could really happen? He could say no, and we'd just pretend it never happened. I could do that. I could *totally* do that.

As hyped up as I was going to get, I left my bedroom and headed for the living room where I could hear the TV playing. Coming around the corner, I found James sitting on the couch, trying to stuff an entire slice of pizza into his mouth in one bite.

I burst into laughter. "Dude, what the hell are you doing? Just take a bite like a normal person." I dropped onto the couch next to him, already feeling more confident.

Instead of responding, as his mouth was full of pizza, James just lifted his hand and gave me the finger. I shook my head at him, ignoring his rude gesture and looking to see what he was watching. Of course, it was the most recent season of *Is It Cake?*

As soon as I watched the first season, I knew James would love it, too, so I got him hooked on it. James would often bake in his free time, and whenever my brother Ezra—who had just finished pastry school—came over, the two of them wouldn't shut up about whatever new technique they were onto at the moment.

"I told you to watch this months ago! You're only watching it now?"

James mumbled something through his mouthful, and I just glared at him in response. He knew I hated that. If his mouth wasn't too full to do it, he would definitely be giving me a shit-eating grin right now. He chewed it more and then took a drink of water to wash down the last of it.

"I honestly forgot about it until I was scrolling for something to watch and it popped up."

"It's good, right?"

"Oh yeah. Grace's cake in the second episode was incredible."

"But nothing will ever beat Johnny Cakes," we said at the same time, turning to look at each other, and bursting into laughter.

"Did you see that cartoon cake he made on his Instagram? I really want to try it!" he said.

I smiled at the enthusiasm in his voice, knowing he would probably make a pretty decent one. "You should do it! Maybe for Will's birthday? It's coming up soon."

"Maybe I will," James said, picking up a napkin and wiping the pizza sauce from the sides of his mouth.

I noticed he had changed his nails, now painted a sparkly black. "Ooo, I like the new nail color."

He looked down, taking it in like he had forgotten. "Oh, yeah. The old one was mostly chipped off, so I redid them earlier."

"Nice." I nodded my head, trailing off into an awkward silence. I felt like James could tell there was something I wanted to ask, but like always, he let me get there on my own time. I tried to figure out the best way to open the conversation, but there was no way forward but through, was there?

"So, remember the conversation we had the other night?"

James froze, another slice of pizza halfway to his mouth. "You mean when I came home and found you crying to *The Princess Bride* yet again?" he teased, mischief twinkling in his eyes.

"Excuse you, I was not *crying*. I was *moping*. There's a difference."

"Mm–hmm," he hummed unconvincingly. It only took a moment to realize he had done it yet again, teased me out of my discomfort.

I took a deep breath to ground myself, knowing that if I didn't just do it, I would end up chickening out. It was now or never.

"Well, remember how I told you the reason I had writer's block and how I tried to hook up with a stranger?" The words squeaked out of me.

He froze, which made my nerves start to come back. "Yes?"

"I realized that I was never going to be able to have sex with a total stranger." Some of the tension eased from James's shoulders as I spoke, and it gave me the confidence to continue. But the nerves still made the words come out of my mouth faster and faster as I blurted out, "I was wondering if instead you would have sex with me?"

10

James

You're My Best Friend - Queen

THERE WAS NO WAY I heard that right. *Right?* Did Nikki fucking Stone actually just ask me to sleep with her? I must have fallen asleep on the couch, and now I was dreaming. That was the only possible explanation. Nikki had never once shown even an ounce of interest in me.

She started chewing on her lip, the most obvious sign of nerves with her, and I snapped out of my daze, blinking at her through my glasses.

I had to clear my throat twice before any words could actually come out. "Did you... Did you just ask me to have sex with you?"

"Um, yes?" An anxious laugh huffed out of her, and she looked down at her lap.

"Can I, uh, ask why?" I tried to school the shock out of my expression, but never in a million years could I have dreamt up this scenario.

She seemed to steel herself before she answered, and my heart ached for her. I never liked seeing her in distress. "I want to start off by saying that if you say no, I promise I'll never bring it up and we can pretend like this never happened." She chuckled awkwardly before continuing. "I really thought about what you said the other might, about how it just needs to be the right person for me. It needs to be someone that feels safe to me, who understands me and my demisexuality. And well, that's pretty much you."

The breath caught in my throat, hearing the words I'd always wanted to hear from her, but not in the way I wanted. But I forced myself to stay silent so she could say everything she needed to first. "There's definitely some assumption here on my side, but I was thinking that since you seem to be OK with and enjoy sex with people you aren't attracted to, and have a super casual approach to it, maybe that same mentality could apply to me? That you could like, teach me. You know, give me 'sex lessons,' as it were?"

Nikki looked up at me through her lashes as she finished speaking, taking in my expression, which I kept carefully neutral. Inside, I was falling apart.

My first thought was *Yes. Yes, Nikki, I want to make love to you.* And that was exactly why I shouldn't, *couldn't* say yes. How could I sleep with her and not fully fall in love with her? If I wasn't already. I feel like part of me had started falling in love with her the moment I met her. But it was all the little things over the past year that had made me fall more and more.

But it wasn't something I was brave enough to act on. Not when she was such an important person in my life. I had casual sex because I enjoyed sex. And it was easy for me to sleep with people I wasn't attracted to, especially when I knew I wasn't going to fall for them.

I turned my body fully towards her, knowing I needed to find the best way to say this so I didn't hurt her feelings. "Nikki, you're one of my best friends," I began. Immediately she started retreating in her shell, and I reached forward to hold her hands. "I value you and our relationship so much, and I wish this was something I could help you with. I just don't know how to do this in a way that won't change our friendship forever."

She was looking down so I couldn't see her face, but the way she curled into herself indicated she was hurt.

"Yeah, no, I totally understand." She sniffed, pulling her hands out of my grasp and leaning away from me. As much as I wanted to her her in my arms, tell her I was wrong and we could do this, I just couldn't. And it was killing me. But I wanted to respect her space and her feelings.

"Nikki, I promise this has nothing to do with you, it's all me. I just—"

"It's OK, I promise," Nikki cut me off, finally looking up at me, and my heart sank at how glassy her eyes were. "Like I said, we can just pretend this never happened, and go back to how things were." She shot me a watery smile, getting up and heading back to her room before I could get another word out.

I buried my face in my hands, fighting back my own tears and wishing this could be different.

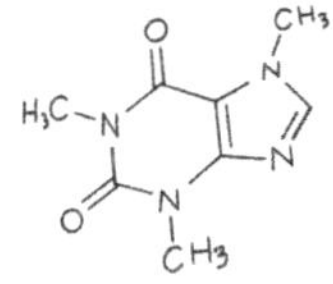

IT HAD ONLY BEEN a day, but it felt like forever, because things were nowhere near back to normal. Nikki was doing her absolute best to ignore me as much as she could. She'd been hiding away in her room the whole time, only coming out for food or the bathroom.

I had no idea how to fix things between us, and no idea how to move forward. Part of me was still kicking myself for not just saying yes. But I also had to respect how she had to protect herself. And if that was by distancing herself for now, I just had to be ok with that.

Walking in the door now, I braced myself for more awkward interactions. It had been a long, rough shift today, and I didn't know if I had it in me to pretend like every-thing wasn't ruined between us. Coming farther into the apartment, I found Nikki and Will on the couch watching a movie.

Nodding my head at them, I walked past to my room to change. Shucking off my jeans, I pulled on a pair of gray sweatpants. My hair was damp with sweat from all the running around I had done, and I raked my hand through the strands, pushing them back from my face. I took a quick look in the mirror and noticed the stubble on my chin. I really did need a shave soon before it turned into a full-on beard.

I took my glasses off, leaving them on my dresser before heading out into the living room to join the three of them. Nikki was curled up in one corner of our giant couch, Will in the middle, leaving the opposite end of the couch from her vacant. I flopped into the spot, kicking my socked feet up onto the coffee table.

Nikki's eyes tracked me as I moved, and I could've sworn they traveled down my body and back up again, but my eyes were too blurry without my glasses to notice for sure. My eyesight was just bad enough that I needed them out and about, but not so bad that I needed them full-time, so I often left them off when I was just hanging around the apartment.

"What're we watching?"

"Some random rom-com that popped up on Netflix," Will responded. "Their movies are often better and worse than Hallmark at the same time, I swear." Will filled me in on what I had missed in the story. After that, we all fell into a comfortable silence, watching the couple break up so that they could have their big grand gesture moment.

"Alright, resident romance expert. On a level of one to ten, how was that grand gesture?" Will asked Nikki after the credits started rolling.

She rubbed her chin in exaggerated thought. "Hmmm, not terrible, but could use more groveling. Six out of ten."

"Fair enough," he responded through a yawn, stretching his arms over his head. "And on that note, it is definitely time for bed."

I stayed slouched in my spot, scrolling on my phone. I was too wired for sleep, and wanted to give Nikki a chance to sneak out of the room without me noticing, but she stayed on the couch. After a few more moments, I finally looked up to see she was twisting her fingers around in her lap, chewing on that damn lip again, a contemplative look on her face.

"You alright, Nik?" I asked softly, as if trying not to spook a wild animal. This was the first time she had willingly stayed in the same room with me since our conversation. I didn't want to get my hopes up that she was finally ready to speak to me again, but I couldn't help the way my heart soared with hope.

"Yeah." She finally looked up at me, smiling softly. "I just wanted to talk with you, if that's alright?"

"Yeah, of course!" I tried to keep my voice from being too cheerful, but I didn't know how successful I was.

"I'm sorry I was avoiding you, I just—"

"No, please, don't worry about it. You take all the time you need," I said, giving her an encouraging nod. *I missed you* is what I didn't say, not sure she was ready to hear it yet.

"I've thought a lot about what you said, and I think you're right. I love our friendship too, and if you think sleeping together would jeopardize it, I don't want to do that. You're so important to me."

My shoulders loosened, feeling like I could finally breathe for the first time since yesterday afternoon. "Good, I'm so glad to hear that."

I tried to keep the smile from my face, but hearing that she cared so deeply for me, even if it wasn't in the way I wish she did, made me the happiest I had been all week.

She continued, "I also just wanted to let you know that my plan hasn't changed." She chewed on her lip once more before pushing her shoulders back.

My heart stalled. "What do you mean?"

"I mean," Nikki said, finally looking up at me and making eye contact, "that I'm still going to find someone else to sleep with."

11

NIKKI

Let's Talk About Sex - Salt-N-Pepa

JAMES STARED AT ME, blinking slowly. It took him a moment, but finally he pulled himself together enough to ask, "I thought you said you knew you couldn't go through with it with a stranger?"

I had said that. And I had also spent the past day trying my best not to cry after being completely rejected by James. I may not have feelings for him beyond our friendship, but rejection of any kind was always extremely difficult for me. My nervous system just couldn't tell the difference between someone saying no one time versus someone saying they hated me.

And while it had gotten better since getting diagnosed with ADHD and understanding there was a reason behind the way I felt things, it didn't stop me from feeling them. Hence, me avoiding him like the plague while I licked my wounds and tried to figure out how to move on from this. I knew that his decision didn't say anything about how he felt about me as a person—it was just a boundary he had to set for himself, and I had to respect that.

But I also knew that I still had a book to write and writer's block to break, with no other ideas as to how to fix it. I was on a tight deadline and had no time to waste, which meant I needed a solution *yesterday*. I also needed to put him out of his misery. Even as I had avoided him, I had noticed him moping around the apartment like a sad puppy, and I hated that I was the one who made him feel like that. I needed to be a big girl and put it behind us. I told him we could pretend like it had never happened, and I meant that.

Taking a deep breath, I said, "Well, I've been thinking more about it. And I think if I get to know someone for more than five minutes this time and don't try to hook up in a bar bathroom"—I smiled wryly—"I'll be OK. Maybe I'll try a dating app this time or something, I don't know. But I needed to tell you that I'm sorry for avoiding you, and I promise I'm all good now."

James didn't say anything, his eyes skipping around my face, brows slightly scrunched together. God, I wish I could tell what he was thinking.

"So, yeah. I told you we could pretend it never happened, so let's just do that. Are we all good?" I asked.

I waited anxiously for his response, hoping he wasn't too upset with me, and that we really could go back to the way things were. It took him a moment, but he seemed to pull himself together, finally responding, "Yes, yes, of course. You know I value our friendship so much. I never want to hurt you."

The tension that had wrung my body so tight since our conversation finally released, and I slumped in my seat.

"So, uh, what did you have in mind for this endeavor? I didn't ask you last time."

I froze at his question, surprised he still wanted to talk about it. "I hadn't really thought that far ahead, to be honest. I just wanted to get it over with." Wow, I really hadn't put much thought into my plan beyond asking him if he was even interested. Burying my face in my hands to cover my embarrassment, I peeked at him between my fingers to see he was staring at me in amusement. "I guess I should sort that out before I try to get someone else to sleep with me, huh?"

He smiled in return. "Yeah, maybe some semblance of a plan would help. You know, like knowing exactly what you want out of it. What your expectations are."

I dropped my hands, finally making real eye contact with him. His hazel eyes bored into me, and I felt like he could actually see into my mind with how intense they were. They looked more green than usual today, pulled out by the forest green button-down he was wearing open over a white tank. Overwhelmed, I looked away. "Yeah, I'll make sure I think about that before I ask someone then."

His voice cut through the air between us, firm and just this side of demanding. "Don't."

I straightened in surprise, "Don't what?"

"Don't ask anyone else."

I furrowed my brow in confusion. "I told you, I don't really have any other ideas on how else to get past this wr—"

"I know." James rested his elbows on his knees, folding his hands between them and looking down at them. He took a deep breath. "I changed my mind."

I opened and closed my mouth, but no sound came out. Clearing my throat, I finally croaked out, "You... you changed your mind?"

"Yes." He met my gaze, and a zing traveled through my body at the intensity in his eyes. "I'll do it."

I gulped in air. Was he serious? "I don't want you to feel forced or anything. I promise I'll be OK asking someone else."

"I know," he responded, voice steady. "You can do whatever you put your mind to. But you're right, it'll be better with someone you feel comfortable with. Besides, who am

I to turn down sex?" James grinned. While it didn't look forced, it didn't look totally natural either.

"Are you sure?" The words came out much breathier than I meant them to, but I had no idea what was happening. Why had he suddenly changed his mind?

His smirk turned reassuring when he saw how concerned I was. Reaching out, he gripped my hands in his. "I promise, I wouldn't be saying yes if I wasn't OK with it. Besides, what's a little sex between friends?"

I laughed, the tension between us breaking. I shifted in my seat, a weird combination of anticipatory arousal and awkwardness coursing through me. This was real. It was actually going to happen, and there was no turning back from this. It would either be the worst or best decision ever, and only time would tell.

I shot him a shy smile. "OK, so we're doing this."

James

WHAT THE FUCK HAD I just done?

I was lying in bed, hands behind my head, staring at the ceiling and contemplating all of my life choices. I hadn't known I was going to change my mind, but when she told me that she was going to ask someone else instead... I just couldn't bear the thought of it.

And it wasn't just the idea of her being with someone else, though I couldn't deny the thought left me sick to my stomach. Mostly, though, I hated the thought of Nikki pushing herself to sleep with someone she wasn't comfortable with. I know she was perfectly capable of making her own decisions, and if she said she was ok with it, then she was. But she had also point-blank told me she would rather it be me. That did things to me I wasn't yet ready to admit to myself.

Something had just come over me, staring at her in that fucking lemon dress I lost my mind over every time she wore, and before I knew what I was doing I had told her not to ask someone else. And now we were going to have sex. My dick started to harden just at the thought. God, I had no idea what to do with myself. Of course I wanted to fuck her. But I was also terrified of what would happen afterwards. I couldn't let myself fall the rest of the way in love with her. I needed her in my life, and our friendship was too important to me to risk.

I also realized that in my haste we hadn't actually talked about where or when or how she wanted to do this. I assumed soon since this was all about her deadline. I was too chicken to go back out and ask her, so instead I pulled out my phone, shooting her a text.

So…

side eye emoji

We probably should have talked about when you wanted to do this.

Oh shit, you're right *anxious grin emoji*

How does one schedule a sex lesson?

Lol, no clue. When is the next time Will and Collins will be out all night? I'm assuming you don't want to tell them.

Ummmm

Collins goes on his next 48hr on saturday, right?

Yeah, is there a game saturday night?

Lol, nice joke. You think I know when sportsball games are?

Lmao, good point

Ok, I just googled it, and yes there is

Ok, so saturday?

Sounds like a plan

Oh shit, is five days enough time for us to both get tested?

Ahhh, good point.

Just made an appointment for Wednesday. You?

Ok, me too.

Saturday, then *salute emoji*

You are such a dork, lol

gif of Stephanie from Full House saying "How rude"

Nikki reacted with a laughing face to my gif, and I stared down at my phone, the smile on my face way too big.

I was in so much trouble.

12

NIKKI

THE NEXT FIVE DAYS passed by in a blur. James and I went back to pretending like everything was normal—joking around with Will and Collins, hanging out in the living room, going to work as usual.

But every time I made eye contact with him, I blushed, and every time he looked at me it felt like he was setting me on fire with his eyes. It was Saturday morning now, and I was pacing back and forth in my room, freaking the fuck out. Last night, all four of us had sat down to do our weekly Friday night binge of our favorite reality dating show with a bunch of hot single people coupling up in a tropical paradise, performing ridiculous challenges, and being the most extra people on the planet. It was the episode where they dressed up in lingerie trying to get each other's heart rates up.

James and I sat next to each other, and I spent the entire episode squirming in my seat. The combination of the episode, the anticipation for tonight, and the way my arm kept brushing against James's had me so horny I'd had to run to my room as soon as it was over to take care of the problem myself. I could have sworn as I left the living room James's eyes were smoldering at me, but when I looked back again he was just joking with the boys.

Normally, when I masturbated I didn't think of anyone in particular, and more so just imagined a sexual act it–self. But last night James's face had popped into my mind against my will. That heated look in his eyes was all I could see as I fell over the edge. I had laid in bed after-wards, catching my breath and praying I hadn't made any noises.

And now, it was time. Collins had left for the start of his shift in the morning before I woke up, and Will was about to head out to the radio station to cover the game. James and I had both gotten our test results back and made sure we had condoms on hand. And now there was nothing to do but wait.

I had spent the day cleaning my room up—and by that, I meant moving the piles of crap into hidden spaces like bed–side drawers and behind closet doors. Now I was sitting on the bed with the TV on, but I didn't even know what was playing. I was lowkey freaking out, scrolling on my phone without even seeing what I was looking at. Was I really about to have sex for the first time, and with one of my closest friends?

Just the anticipation had me both wet and so anxious I felt like I was going to vibrate out of my own skin. More time must have passed than I realized, because before I knew it, there was a knock at my bedroom door. I leapt out of the bed, looking down at my phone to see it had been an hour already—even though it had only felt like ten minutes.

I took in my clothing and realized I was still wearing my oversized, stained-but-oh-so-comfortable sweats and a shirt that definitely needed to be washed. I had meant to change earlier, but lost track of time.

"Just a minute!" My voice was much higher-pitched than it should have been, and I cleared my throat as I scrambled to my closet to throw something at least a little nice on. Thank god I was already wearing a matching bra and panty set. It was nude and unlined, the shades of my nipples just barely visible through the floral-patterned tight-knit mesh fabric. Wait, should I be wearing only my underwear when I opened the door for him?

God, how did people do this normally?

Deciding on a simple floral cotton minidress—cute but not looking like I was trying too hard—I finally opened the door.

"Hey." It came out way too breathy after running around my room like a chicken with its head cut off.

James smiled, raising a brow at me. "You good?"

I took him in, his tan, ribbed-knit polo tucked into black slacks. "Oh, you know. Business as usual."

"Ah, yes. Do this often then?"

"Psh." I waved a hand. "Of course. I hook up with my friends all the time."

We both broke into laughter at that, and some of the tension eased between us. I opened the door wider, waving him into my room. He walked in, looking around and taking everything in, like he hadn't been in here plenty of times before.

I chewed my lip, leaning back against the closed door as I watched him. The room was dead silent, and I felt like if I made a noise, everything would come crumbling down around us.

James turned to look at me, and when he saw how tense I was, his whole body softened as he walked towards me. "We don't have to do this, NikNak. I can help you figure out some other way to get past this writer's block."

I was already shaking my head before he finished speaking, "No. No, I need to do this. I *want* to do this, I promise. I'm just... I'm nervous and awkward and—"

"It's ok." He reached out, tucking a piece of hair behind my ear. The breath shuddered out of me as the tips of his fingers grazed my cheek. He planted that hand on the door next to my head, leaning in closer until all I could feel was the heat radiating from his body. "Where do you want to start?" he asked, his voice low, my eyes stuck on the movement of his lips.

I tried to speak, but nothing came out. His scent—some mix of sweet with an undercurrent of sharp and spicy—clouded my brain. I gulped, trying again. "I, uh, I don't know. What do you think?" My gaze drifted back up his face until I met his eyes, heat blazing in them.

"How about this?" He moved his hand back from the door, sliding it into my hair until it cradled the back of my head. He waited for my nod of permission before continuing, his other hand coming to the side of my face, using his thumb to tilt my chin up until my mouth was angled towards his.

And then, ever so slowly, he leaned down to me until our lips were touching. It was a whisper of a sensation, the softest brush of his lips against mine before he pulled back the slightest amount. Just a moment, before going back in again, firmer this time. And then all at once, he was kissing me.

His lips moved against mine, warm and soft and sure. The kiss was slow and sensual, and I found myself slowly beginning to reciprocate until I was fully kissing him back. My hands rose up until they were resting at his waist. He hummed in approval, and then, feeling brave, I dragged them up his sides until they were sliding up his chest. He moaned into my mouth. The sound went straight to my core, and I clenched in a combination of surprise and arousal.

The kiss turned fiercer and I felt him lick at my lips, seeking entrance. I opened my mouth to him, and then his tongue was sweeping into my mouth. The first thing I noticed was the rich flavors of coffee and chocolate. I melted further into him at the taste. That bastard knew mochas were my favorite; he must have drunk one right before coming in here.

I felt his smile against my mouth and I knew he knew exactly what he was doing. And that was when James *really* started kissing me. His tongue dove into my mouth, stroking along my own as he angled his head to kiss me deeper. The hand that had been cradling the back of my head changed to grip my hair instead, pulling it just enough for the slightest sting, sending tingles scattering across my scalp, and a whimper escaped my throat. How he knew I found that soothing was beyond me, but I was too far gone to question it. In turn, I slid my hands from his chest up and around until they could dive into his hair. It was thick, and so soft.

I had never felt so turned on by a kiss before. It wasn't butterflies—or at least I didn't think so, since I didn't know what they felt like. I hadn't been sexually attracted to anyone before, and I still wasn't attracted to James now. But something about the comfort of this moment allowed my mind to relax enough for me to simply enjoy the act of kissing itself. In a place I was familiar with, with a person who made me feel safe, one of my favorite flavors on his tongue.

I was so lost in the moment of it all, getting wetter and wetter, that I didn't notice his hand was sliding up my thigh. All at once I felt his cold fingertips brush up and across the outside of my thigh to the inside. I gasped into his mouth in surprise at the unexpected, unfamiliar sensation. My heart pounded furiously in my chest, and I faltered against his mouth, my hands slipping from his hair.

His hand paused for a moment before fully retreating from my thigh, coming to rest gently on my waist instead. I tried to keep kissing him as I had been, putting my hands on his waist in return, but my mind had begun to wander, thinking about what would come after the kiss. And then my heart began racing for a whole different reason, as I began to panic at the thought of taking it from kissing to actual sex.

As my body slowly began tensing against my will, my kissing faltered again, and James pulled back, brows crinkled as his eyes scanned rapidly across my face. "Nikki? What's wrong? Are you OK? Did I do something you aren't comfortable with?"

My heart soared at the concern he felt for me, how his first and immediate thought was to make sure that he was wrong and hadn't crossed any of my boundaries. I smiled shakily at him. "It's OK, I'm OK."

"You don't seem alright," he replied, examining me closer. "You're stiff as a board and flinching while I kiss you. Please, just tell me if I did anything wrong. I have to know you can communicate with me if we do this and that you'll tell me to stop if you want me to. I know you're nervous about this, but we still need to make sure we're communicating."

James was right. I needed to be able to communicate what I did and didn't like, to keep both of us feeling safe and cared for. "I just wasn't expecting your hand, and it was colder than I expected, and then I couldn't stop thinking about your hand traveling higher and what would come after that and I just—"

"Shhh." He shushed me soothingly, rubbing his hands up and down my arms. "It's OK. Nikki, we don't have to have sex tonight."

I pulled further away from him, voice shaky as I asked, "You're changing your mind again?"

13

NIKKI

PHYSICAL – OLIVIA NEWTON JOHN

"No," he rushed to say. "No, I'm just saying, why don't we stop and make a plan for what exactly you want out of this, and how many times you wanna get together." I took a deep breath, relaxing at his words. "I promise, I'm in this with you. I just want to be as comfortable as possible. I want you to enjoy this as much as I know I will."

The words washed through me, calming the sting that had already begun. James wasn't rejecting me; he was just trying to move at my pace. I closed my eyes and leaned my head against his chest, letting him wrap his arms around me, rubbing his hands in soothing circles on my back.

"I'm sorry." I spoke the muffled words into his shirt. James rested his chin on my head, holding me tighter. It's something all the guys knew, that in times of distress, pressure always helped calm me down faster.

"Why are you sorry?" James murmured back.

"Because I'm always so... much. So emotional, so reactive, so chaotic."

"Hey." James pulled back, cradling my face in his hands. "You're never anything but perfectly you." I felt heat rising to my cheeks at his words. He tracked my reaction with his eyes, crinkled at the corners now with amusement. "You never could take a compliment, could you?"

I huffed a laugh, pushing at his chest halfheartedly. He stumbled back, clutching his chest, a grin on his face as he sat on the edge of my bed. "So what do we do now?" I joined him on the bed.

James turned to me, pulling one knee up onto the bed, and I mirrored him.

"Well," he began contemplatively, "I know you said you wanted to have sex, but what *exactly* is it you want to get out of this?"

My brows scrunched in confusion. "What do you mean?"

"Do you just want to bang it out, one and done? And if so, what kind of sex did you want to experience? Hands, oral, penetration? All of those are different types of sex we could have."

"Oh," I replied, my heart racing again, but for a different reason. Hearing him lay it all out like that should have felt more clinical than sexy, but I found myself getting aroused again as I pictured all the different options. I realized I should have been asking him the same. "Um, well, first, are there any boundaries that you have?"

"NikNak, I don't think there's anything you could think up that would cross my boundaries." The glint in his eyes had me squirming where I sat, a fresh wave of wetness coating my panties.

I shot him back a challenging look. "Oh yeah? So you'd be down for me to peg you then?" I had no idea where the boldness came from, but I just liked pushing his buttons as much as he seemed to.

James licked his lips, readjusting himself in his pants while keeping eye contact with me and my core clenched. When he spoke, his voice was pure sin. "Oh, darling, you have no idea how much I would enjoy that."

Fuck. Well, that had backfired.

I tried speaking, but my throat was so dry I had to swallow and try again. "Okay, you're probably right about that then."

"I'm always right. It's what makes me so awesome," James looked way too smug as he spoke, and I simply glared at him until he broke into laughter. "OK, OK, I'm kidding. Just not about the pegging." He winked.

"I guess I need to think about what I want to do then," I replied.

The grin on his face subsided into something softer, more real. "Once you think of what exactly you want to do, I'm happy to do whatever you want. I promise." James lifted his pinky finger, and I reached up to wrap my own around it.

"Thank you, James," I replied. "For everything. I really mean it."

Releasing his pinky from mine, he leaned back on the bed, resting on his elbows. "So, do you have any ideas of what you want? Do you want me to come up with ideas with you, or do you want me to leave and you tell me later?"

I took a moment to think about it. The idea of talking about it made me squirmy and not in a good way, but James had the experience I didn't, which is why I'd asked him to help me in the first place. My face flaming, I tried to be brave and forged on. "Would you help me?"

James smiled. "I would love nothing more. Now, come here, lie down and stargaze with me. I know it's easier to not make eye contact during awkward conversations." He fully collapsed to his back, tucking his hands under his head. Most of the tension eased from my body at how well he knew me. With a smile of my own, I did as told, lying back and folding my hands over my rounded stomach, staring up at the glow in the dark stars on my ceiling.

"So, what's the goal here?"

"To get past my writer's block and finish writing my book."

"No, that's the *result* you're looking for. What is it you actually want to try? Just penetrative sex? Or do you want to explore?"

I paused, caught off guard with his question. To be honest, I hadn't thought through what I wanted past "get fucked and no longer be a virgin trying to write a smutty romance book." While I thought the idea of virginity was just heteronormative purity culture bullshit to control women and their bodies, I still sometimes felt the stigmatization around it. But yeah, I may have gone into this impulsively, with no thought-out plan. ADHD strikes again.

"I probably should have thought about this before diving in, huh?" I replied wryly.

"Maybe," James hedged. "But also, maybe it's a good thing we're talking it through together and setting clear expectations and boundaries for both of us. For instance," he sounded uncertain for the first time in this entire interaction, which piqued my interest, "I do have one boundary I'd like to discuss."

"Of course," I rushed to reply. "Anything." What could James, who was always confident in his sexual exploits, be nervous about?

"This is purely physical. I can't— I can't do any relationship-type things. Casual sex between friends is never an unmessy thing, so we can't catch feelings. Is that OK?"

"Agreed," I immediately responded. "Just physical."

"Alright, now that we've gotten that down, what else? I know you say this is just for the book, but what about *you?* Is there anything you want to try?"

I was very thankful in this moment that he wasn't looking at me, as I was sure my face was redder than Clifford at the moment. Talking about my sexual fantasies with anyone wasn't a thing I did, *ever*. But I had to keep reminding myself that James was right, and we needed to be able to fully communicate about everything related to what we were doing.

"Um, well, I guess at the very least all the basics?"

"And the basics would be..."

"You would know that better than me!"

"Ah, ah, ah. That's assuming, and the 'basics' of sex as most people have historically referred to are cis-norma-tive and queer-exclusionary."

"OK, *professor*, if you're gonna make me spell it out for you."

James let out a tortured groan. "Don't call me that." His face was scrunched up like he was in pain, and I was confused for a moment until my eyes flicked down to where his dick was tenting his pants.

"Ooo, does someone have a professor kink then?"

"Nikki, please." His voice was strained, and I decided to take pity on him.

Laughing, I replied, "Fine, fine. By the basics, I mean like the main three things I guess. Hands, oral, and penetration. And before you say it, I do mean you penetrating me, not me pegging you."

"Damn, OK." I could hear the grin in his voice. "Any specific positions you're curious about?"

I took a moment to think about it and also to gather myself. The more we talked about, the more turned on I was getting. I could feel my nipples pushing at the fabric of my bra, the ache at the apex of my thighs getting harder to ignore. *Not the only thing getting* harder *to ignore*, I thought to myself, glancing again at the impressive erection James had going on.

"Um, probably doggy-style? I've heard that most people find that more, uh, pleasurable." At this point I wouldn't be surprised if my face was hot enough to start a fire.

"Alright, we can do that." I could tell from his voice that he was struggling just as much as I was. "How, uh, how slow would you like to go? Maybe we break it up into lessons? Do one thing each time and slowly build up?"

"Yeah, yeah, that works for me." My voice came out so breathy it was barely more than a whisper.

"OK, well, I guess I'll head to my room now. Just let me know when you're ready to try again, and we'll find a time Will and Collins are gone again." At his words, I felt a pang of disappointment in my chest. I knew now that I wasn't ready to jump all the way in on the first go, but I also didn't like the thought of leaving off like this. Besides, I was still horny as fuck, and obviously so was he. Maybe we could just start *really* slow right now.

The words were out of my mouth before I had truly decided to speak. "Don't go."

14

James

Take Me to Church - Hozier

I froze at Nikki's words. I had been fully prepared to leave before she spoke—just because I was so horny I could cry didn't make it her job to help me deal with it. I was just going to go back to my room and jerk myself into oblivion. But now she *didn't* want me to leave?

I'd been trying so hard this whole time not to look at her at all. Not only to let her have the privacy she needed to feel comfortable enough to talk about this, but also because seeing her tits in that dress might have made me spontaneously combust in my pants.

At the movement, though, I finally allowed myself to look at her. She was flushed from her cheeks all the way down to her chest, which was moving up and down faster than normal. Thank god she was just as affected as me. Before I could ask her what she was doing, she got up to her knees and swung one leg over until she was straddling me.

"What are you doing?" The words came out like I'd just had the wind knocked out of me, but it was taking all of my strength not to thrust up into her warm center. With her in a dress, the only things between us were my pants and boxers and her panties. I could feel the warmth of her through the layers of fabric as she settled herself on my rock-hard cock with a sigh.

"Say the word and I'll get back off, I promise." Nikki's eyes were glazed over with lust. "But now that I feel more in control, now that I know our clothes aren't coming off tonight and I'm not overthinking everything, all I can think about is how I'm so turned on it hurts. And from what I can tell"—she gave the barest roll of her hips, a whimper escaping her throat as my head fell back to the bed, my eyes slamming shut as I forced myself to stay still—"you're just as desperate as me. Instead of taking care of this on our own, I figured we could find a little mutual satisfaction. Is that OK?"

"God, yes." I surged up, pulling her head down to mine at the same time, but she stopped my with a hand to my chest. I froze, wondering fi she had changed her mind, but all she did was reach for my face and gently pulled my glasses off my face, setting them gently on the bedside table. And then *finally*, she pulled me back to her and our mouths crashed together. We moaned in unison as the kiss immediately turned desperate, and she began to *finally* roll her hips against mine. Pure bliss flooded my body as my dick finally received the pressure it had been aching for. I wasn't going to last very long, not with how much anticipation and build-up had left me leaking into my boxers.

I gripped her hips firmly, pushing her even harder against me. Her mouth separated from mine on a gasp, head falling back as she fell into a rhythm. I took advantage of the perfect angle to kiss and lick my way up to her ear, pulling the lobe into my mouth and biting down hard enough to sting but not to mark.

Nikki cried out in pleasure, and I realized my theory from our first kiss was right. She'd made a similar noise when I had pulled her hair the slightest bit. My girl liked a little pain with her pleasure. Wait, no. *Not* my girl. Nikki. Nikki was not mine, and I could not let myself forget that.

Shaking that thought off, I got back to the gorgeous woman grinding on my dick. I needed to appreciate every moment I had with her this way.

"Mmm, you liked that, did you?"

She nodded her head frantically, too far gone for words.

"Can I touch your tits, Nikki? Over the clothes only, I promise."

"Please," she cried, her hips moving faster, faltering in rhythm as the pleasure began to overtake her.

As I lowered my head to her breasts, her hands dove into my hair, gripping and lightly pulling at it, and my cock jumped, more pre-cum leaking into my boxers. I wasn't going to last much longer, and I refused to come before she did. Keeping one hand on her hips to help her continue grinding on me, I raised the other one to stroke up the side of her breast.

They weren't the biggest tits I'd ever worked with, but they weren't small either, filling the full span of my palm. I brushed my thumb across the surface, searching for her nipple through the fabric of her bra and dress. Once I found it, I lowered my head to take it into my mouth. I opened my lips wide until I had the entire tip in my mouth, laving my tongue against the stiff bud.

Nikki whimpered again, her hands pulling more firmly at my hair. "God, I'm so close, James," she cried out. I could hear the desperation in her voice, knew how badly she needed to come, because I needed the same. Her hips hit just right, and I moaned into her skin.

"What do you need, Nikki? Use your words." I licked across her chest, dipping my tongue into the valley between her tits as she whimpered again. God, I couldn't wait to see her naked.

She stopped moving and I almost cried, so desperate for release, but then I realized what she was doing. She pushed the sleeves of her dress down her arms until it fell around her waist, leaving her only in her bra.

"I thought you said no clothes coming off? And before that brain of yours gets any ideas, I am not at all opposed to this," I added quickly when I saw her begin to falter.

She smiled at me then, and I almost came in my pants from that alone. It was so bright and unfiltered and just the slightest bit crooked. Oh, I was so fucked when it came to her. But I didn't even care anymore.

"Just this," she panted, beginning to moving her hips again, head falling back once more. "My nipples aren't very sensitive," she continued, and I nearly swallowed my tongue when she raked her fingernails across my scalp, a bolt of lightning shooting straight down to my cock. The only thing stopping me from coming was biting down on my lip so hard I could taste blood. "I needed your mouth closer to my skin."

That was all the encouragement I needed, and I dove back in. This time, with the barrier of her dress gone, I could feel the heat of her skin through her bra as I sucked her nipple into my mouth. Her hips began picking up speed, small sighs and breathy moans escaping at every movement.

That's when I bit down on her nipple, hard enough for her to feel my teeth beneath the thin fabric, and she cried out one last time, her entire body seizing in my arms, tensing as her orgasm rolled through her.

Nikki's hips jerked against mine, and I finally let myself go, soothing her nipple with my tongue as I gripped her hips firmly and slammed my still-clothed dick up into her. It only took two or three thrusts before I was soaking my jeans through with cum, a deep groan rumbling from my chest and my head fell forward, resting against the tops of her breasts.

We sat there together panting for what felt like an eternity as we both came back down. I turned my head to the side, planting a soft kiss on the side of her breast before pulling back.

Nikki had a glazed expression on her face, and I tried not to let my ego get the best of me. "Holy shit," she finally said between breaths.

"You can say that again."

"Was that... was that how it normally is for you?"

I licked my lips, stalling while I tried to figure out how to answer. *It's never been like that for me,* I wanted to say. But if I said that, she would know. That what I felt for her was more than platonic. And she didn't want that, not with me.

"Sometimes," I hedged, settling on a half-truth. "There are levels of chemistry outside of attraction. Some people have more chemistry than others, and I guess we have more."

Nikki grinned at me, stroking a thumb across my cheek, and I held myself back from grabbing her and shoving my tongue back in her mouth like I wanted to.

"Well, thank god for that."

15

James

LOVERBOY - A-WALL

I WOKE UP WITH a smile on my face. I had left Nikki's room last night after we finished (pun intended) with a promise to figure out the next time the guys were gone for the first—well, technically second, if you counted what we'd done last night, which we probably should—"lesson." But I had needed to get myself cleaned up before things got stiff in a different, less pleasant way.

I had kissed her on the forehead as I left the room and instantly regretted it. Not because it wasn't nice, but because it was too nice. I was the one who'd said we needed to keep things strictly physical between us, and sweet forehead kisses were the exact opposite of that.

Back in my room, I stripped out of my dirty clothes, before heading to the bathroom. I was still so keyed up that I ended up jerking myself off again in the shower just by picturing what she had looked like on top of me, head thrown back in passion, hair stuck to her forehead with sweat as she rode me to her own pleasure.

Thinking about it now in bed had my morning wood come back to life. My hand drifted down my torso until I was gripping my cock in my hand, stroking myself slowly. This time I imagined what she would taste like when I finally got my mouth on her. It didn't take long until I was coming over my stomach, and I grimaced, looking down at the mess I'd made. The mess Nikki was making of me.

Carefully, I reached over to my nightstand, grabbing a tissue to clean myself up. After I got myself as clean as possible, I looked over at the clock to see it was already one in the afternoon.

The problem with being a bartender was that your body got on weird sleep schedules. When you worked until two or three a.m. most nights, you ended up going to bed a few hours after that, and then all the sudden you were waking up in the afternoon. Getting my ass up, I stumbled into the kitchen, rubbing my eyes and yawning. I popped a pod into the Keurig, pushing the button that brought me the magical juice. I leaned against the counter, scrolling mindlessly on my phone as I waited. I was absolutely useless before coffee. Honestly, at any given time, there was probably more coffee running through my veins than blood.

Unfortunately for me, I had chronic gastritis, and I paid for my caffeine addiction dearly. But most days, the pain was worth it.

I smiled to myself at the memory of the night before. I'm pretty sure Nikki knew exactly why I'd done what I'd done, drinking a mocha right before coming to her door. If I was a coffee connoisseur, she was a coffee goddess. I'm pretty sure there was no blood left in her veins—it was just pure coffee. Familiarity was something that soothed her, and I figured she'd enjoy mocha on my breath more than mint. My hunch definitely paid off.

"Bro, who got you smiling like that?" Will's voice caught me so off guard I threw my phone across the room.

"Jesus, dude, what the fuck!" My heart was galloping in my chest. I looked over, and he was sitting at the table, smirking at me over a bowl of pho on the table in front of him.

"Hey man, I've been here the whole time. It's not my fault you were too busy with your little heart eyes over there to notice me."

I glared at him, walking across the room to pick the phone back up, stomping back over to the Keurig and turning my back to Will.

"Soooo..." His voice dragged the word out teasingly.

"So, what?" I grunted back at him.

"So, who's got you all moony-eyed?"

"I was thinking about my coffee. You know how much I love coffee."

"Nah, you *lust* after coffee. That expression on your face was some sappy shit."

That almost got a smile out of me, and the bastard knew it.

"You're not going to tell *me*, your oldest friend, who you've fallen in love with?! I am so offended."

"You are not my oldest friend, you idiot."

"Now that was just mean." He pouted at me.

"You know my oldest friend is John from high school," I responded pointedly.

Will scoffed, waving a dismissive hand. "He doesn't count. You barely even talk to him anymore."

"You don't count," I mumbled under my breath, even though he was right. My cup of my life juice was finally done brewing so I prepared my coffee. Picking the mug up to bring it to my nose, I huffed a lungful of that rich, decadent mix of chocolate and coffee. I blew on it before taking a sip, not caring that it was still hot enough to burn my tastebuds off, moaning at the swirling flavors on my tongue.

"Damn, dude, get a room." Will shook his head at me, heading back to his seat, slurping down a spoonful of the pho.

"I would if I could," I replied sincerely as I followed behind him, sitting on the opposite side of the table, taking another sip and moaning again. Finally back on this mortal plane, I asked, "How was the game last night?

"So you're human again?" He raised a brow at me.

"Sorry?"

Will just sighed, shaking his head at me like I was a misbehaving puppy. "Apologies don't end in question marks, James."

"Ok, let's try again." I made a whooshing sound, waving my arms stretched out in front of myself.

Will looked at me like I had lost my mind. "What are you doing?"

"Rewinding time to go back before I drank my coffee so I can start over again and not be as big of a dick this time," I said, the tone of my voice implying the *duh*.

"I'm not even gonna engage with all of that." He motioned me, ignoring my antics. "To answer your question," he replied instead, "we won. Actually, it was a pretty good game. Picked it up from a tie in the last quarter. Weren't you gonna watch the game? What did you do instead?"

I almost choked on the sip I had just taken, setting the mug back down, "Yeah, I fell asleep on the couch watching *Is It Cake?* instead." I hoped he didn't catch the lie, and read it as guilt for missing the game instead. I always watched the game if I was home from work and he was reporting.

"You know what, that is so valid. Cake is better than sports any day." Will nodded his head appreciatively, and I grinned back, equal parts relieved and guilt-ridden. I hated lying to him, but I didn't really have a choice with this one.

"Aight, I'm out of here, gotta get back to work." He reached out with his fist, and I tapped it with my own as he walked past, dropping his dishes in the sink. "You working tonight?"

"Yeah, I'll be heading in soon to get some boring busy work done before we open actually."

"Aight, see you tomorrow then."

Nikki

THE SLEEPY SIREN WAS packed tonight. I'd been sitting at home doomscrolling in my room, and had the thought that I should get out of the house. Next thing I knew I was walking into The Sleepy Siren. Why had I decided to come here? And alone, too. No buffer of Will or Collins. No pretense of a roommate outing. Just me going to visit the guy who made me come last night at his place of work.

Part of me didn't even want to see him, didn't think I could handle it yet. It wasn't like we'd even seen each other naked yet, but we had made each other come and I had no idea how to look him in the eye now. I was fully aware that this entire thing was my idea and my doing, and I was sure that I could get over it and act normal around him again. But maybe I needed a minute to reset and get used to this new normal between us.

Oh, god. The more I thought about being here and talking to James, the more I realized that this was a terrible idea, and I needed to leave immediately. But just when I had decided that and turned around to head back out the door, I heard a voice call out.

"Nikki?"

I froze, before turning slowly back around towards the bar, where James was staring at me with a pleasantly surprised look on his face. I gave him a small smile, waving my hand awkwardly at him as I made my way to the bar.

"Hey!" My voice came out all weird, so I cleared my throat. "What's up?"

"What's up?" James raised his brow, his lips twitching. He looked around the room with an exaggerated expression of confusion. "I think I'm at work, but I'm not totally sure?"

"Shut up."

A grin spread across his face. "What are you doing here?"

I shrugged. "Eh, I was bored." The truth was, I couldn't stop thinking about last night, and I'd wanted to see James again. But I had no idea why. Maybe being so vulnerable with someone in a way I never had been before just made me want to seek that person out. I was sure it wasn't anything more than that. It wasn't like I was in love with James all of a sudden.

Sure, I could look at him and admit that he was just straight-up an attractive person. I mean, there was a reason he was so popular, why he had no shortage of people wanting to hook up with him. But I still didn't feel anything when I looked at him. But I also felt myself wanting to be around him. So, here I was.

James smiled brightly at me, opening his mouth "Well, I'm g—" He cut off when a customer yelled at him from down the bar. He rolled his eyes to me, holding up a finger. "Just a minute."

I snickered at him as he walked away, watching as the annoyance fled his face, replaced with a friendly expression. I sat with my elbows on the bar, observing his interactions with the customers, more vying for his attention after the first guy.

It was mesmerizing to watch the ease with which he interacted with people. It never failed to astound me how easily neurotypical people seemed to be able to handle social situations. Especially when I always felt like I was two steps behind in the dark.

The next customer came up to him and was obviously flirting hardcore. I laughed to myself at first, always amused at how much people loved to hit on attractive bartenders. But then James leaned in as well, and he winked at them while he made their drink. I'd seen him flirt back with customers countless times before, but for some reason this time I felt... weird. I did not like it.

I looked away and pulled my phone out to distract myself. What was I even doing here? I rarely ever, if ever at all, came to visit James alone at work. What, one dry-humping session and suddenly I was following him around like a puppy? Jesus, I needed to get a hold of myself.

When James came back, I cleared my throat. "Hey, sorry. I'm actually gonna head out." I swear it looked like James was disappointed for a second, but no, I was just imagining things. I held up my phone. "Noah texted, so I'm gonna go chat with her. But I'll see you at home?" I hated lying to him, but I had no idea how else to get out of here without making it awkward.

He nodded and gave me a soft smile. "Night, Nikki."

I ignored the weird feeling in my stomach as I walked out of the bar.

16

NIKKI

Coming Home - Part II - Skylar Grey

Delete. Delete. Delete.

I dropped my head and banged it repeatedly against my desk. It had been two days since I'd gone to visit James at work. Three days since we humped ourselves into oblivion. I had hoped that even though we hadn't done much, it had been enough to get me started on my writing. But I had spent the last three days sitting in front of my laptop, trying to get words down to no avail. All I had to show for myself was one paragraph, and I didn't even know if iI was going to keep it.

The female main character's friend was helping her get the guy she was in love with to fall for her as well. I'd had the plot in my head since book one, and I had been excited to write it since then. But it just wasn't clicking, and the characters weren't doing what I wanted them to. And that was when I could get any words down at all.

I knew I needed to be writing, that my clock was ticking, but the words were still just out of reach. Deep down I knew that one day, one moment of intimacy, wasn't going to just magically fix me—but you try telling my brain that.

Just thinking about that night with James had my core clenching with need again. I don't know what had come over me to be so bold when I straddled him. Well, that wasn't quite true. I knew it was untamed lust. My need to come had been more than my fear of being so vulnerable. How James knew I needed to be bitten, II had no idea but was more than grateful that he has intuited it.

We still hadn't talked about when we were having the next lesson, partly because of the fact that, besides that random trip to the bar, I had been holed up in my room since then. I wasn't avoiding him; I had just been spending most of my time trying to convince my brain to write something, *anything*. But to be honest, a part of me *was* also probably avoiding him, not ready to confront whatever feeling it was that I had while watching him flirt with customers at the bar.

Besides, we still needed to figure out the next time we'd be home alone. Collins didn't go back on shift for four more days. Unlike me, however, Collins had a very active social life and regularly left the apartment voluntarily, so there was always the possibility of him being out one night between now and then.

I looked down, realizing my screen had gone dark while I'd been staring blankly at it, fantasizing about what it would be like when James really touched me. I blinked at the reflection staring at me.

I looked like I hadn't slept for a week, and I was still wearing the same stained Billie Eilish concert tee I'd put on when I got home from the bar two nights ago. It was a very sad sight, and I knew I needed to step away and come back again with a fresh... everything. I lifted my arm to sniff my armpit—yep, definitely needed to start with a shower.

Picking my phone up to check what day it was, I saw it was a Tuesday. *Perfect.*

Tuesday was family dinner night, and I could use the distraction. Our family was pretty casual, and we had decided on a designated day of the week where anyone who was around was welcomed for a nice home-cooked meal. I didn't go often, due to lack of time awareness, or just not wanting to put on real pants and leave the house, but I really needed it today. I pulled up the family group chat, shooting a message.

Robyn

Omg, she's alive?

Alex

Tbh, I thought she'd just been abducted by aliens or something

Noah

I told you all I saw her last week.

Robyn

Yeah, but you could have just been looking at your reflection and forgot

Noah

unamused emoji

WE AREN'T IDENTICAL

Alex

You sure about that?

Ezra

I'll be there

Thanks for being the only normal one here Ezra

Robyn

Omg, I told you Alex, Nikki is Ezra's favorite, he never makes sure to come when I'm at family dinner

Noah

> You literally live at home, you're there every time dumbass

Robyn

> I'm telling mom you called me that

> Definitely already regretting this decision

My family was a *lot*, but to be fair, so was I. I shook my head, smiling down at my phone as I left my room for the bathroom. One of my biggest ADHD struggles was object permanence. I loved my family more than I could express in words, but when they weren't in front of me, I often forgot about them. It made me feel like a shitty person sometimes, but I wasn't actively choosing to forget about them and I didn't love them any less; my brain was just wired differently.

Especially when I was in my drafting cave. But whenever I did remember to come up for air, my family was always there and waiting for me with open arms.

I turned the shower on, getting my music set up while the water warmed up. I couldn't stand silence and always had either a TV show or more likely music playing in the background. Being left with my own thoughts in silence? Please don't torture me like that.

Back in my room after the shower, I was getting dressed when my phone pinged with a new text. I picked it up, my heart skipping a beat when I saw James's name on the screen.

I swiped the message up, smiling at his text.

Guess who just told me they have a date tomorrow and won't be home?

Let me guess, he's tall and annoying?

Damn, NikNak, you talk about all your friends that way?

Hey, you all know the meaner I am, the more I like you

ANYWAYS

As I was saying, Collins will be out tomorrow night. And isn't there a game tomorrow too?

How many times do I have to remind you I never know when sports are happening

Nerd *eyeroll emoji*

And don't you forget it *winking emoji*

Alright, just confirmed and there is indeed a game tomorrow

> Tomorrow then?

As long as you feel ready.

I have an admin shift tomorrow, I'll be home from the bar around 9

> Tomorrow it is *blushing emoji*

I set my phone down, smiling as I got dressed for family dinner. The smile stayed on my face the entire drive there.

17

NIKKI

I'll Be There For You - The Remembrandts

"—WAS SITTING THERE, YOU dick," Robyn's voice greeted me as I opened the front door.

My mom's voice came next, yelling from the kitchen, "Why do I still have to tell you two to play nice? You are both adults now."

"Barely," I heard Alex's muttered reply as I turned the corner into the living room, finding all of my siblings besides Noah. Alex was seated in the coveted recliner, scrolling on his phone. His tousled dirty blonde hair was just past his ears, green eyes sharp as he scanned whatever he was looking at on his phone. He did swimming all through high school, and still worked out in the pool often. He wasn't huge, but he wasn't exactly small either.

Alex was the middle of the five of us, but he wasn't our brother by blood. He was our cousin on our mom's side, but his parents had died in a car crash when he was just five. It had never been a question about where he belonged, and our parents legally adopted him immediately. He was currently still living at home, having skipped college to try to make it as an actor. So far he'd landed some small theatre roles and a few commercials and roles as an extra, but he was so talented and hardworking that we all had no doubt his big break was around the corner.

Robyn, my youngest sister, was glaring at him from the end of the couch closest to him, her arms crossed over her chest. Her dark brown hair was cut in a shaggy bob right at her chin, and her eyes were a lighter shade of blue than mine, almost icy in color, framed by eyeliner so sharp it would put Taylor Swift to shame.

She was the shortest of the family as well, not stick-thin but not fat either, and her left arm was covered in a sleeve tattoo, just as eclectic as her personality. She had just begun her third year of community college, taking the most random assortment of classes because she couldn't decide what she wanted to major in.

Ezra was on the other end of the couch, his unruly dark brown curls spilling around his face, hiding his bright green eyes. He currently had a full, thick beard going. He was the biggest of us all, tall and fat over muscles, built like a linebacker, with his entire upper body from shoulders to hips covered in tattoos. He was working as a pastry sous chef at a nice restaurant in LA, but his dream was to own a bakery of his own someday.

He had his nose buried in what looked to be a historical romance book. Noah read a romance every now and then, but Ezra was my only other sibling who enjoyed romance books as much as I did. We'd chat about them often, giving each other recommendations.

None of them noticed when I entered. After a moment, I finally said, "What a warm welcome from my loving family."

They finally all looked up, and a chaotic cacophony of noise greeted me as they all got up to embrace me. I laughed and hugged them each back in turn, an ache settling in my chest as I realized just how much I had been missing them without noticing.

I left them in the living room to greet my parents where they were cooking in the kitchen. The moment Mom saw me, she dropped what she was doing to scoop me in her arms. She squeezed me tightly, and I closed my eyes against the tears that suddenly wanted to swell. Sometimes a hug from her was just what I didn't realize I needed.

She pulled back, gripping me by the shoulders as she swept her eyes over me. "Oh, sweet girl, it's been too long!"

"I know." I smiled sheepishly. "I've been so caught up in this draft I haven't been very good at peopling lately."

"We're just glad you could make it this week, bug," Dad said as he came up to me, planting a kiss on my forehead before giving me a tight hug himself.

I cleared my throat, annoyed with how easily I got emotional. It had only been a few weeks since I'd seen them. I needed to get a grip. "So, what's for dinner?" I asked.

"It's your lucky night, we're making your favorite." Mom winked at me, going back to stir the soup bubbling on the stove.

"Omg, it's been ages since I've had French onion." I leaned over the pot, taking in a deep sniff and moaning at the deliciously rich aroma. I looked over at the other pan on the stove, seeing one of my dad's famous homemade grilled cheese sandwiches crisping up. My mouth watered at the combination of smells, my stomach rumbled, and I realized just how hungry I was. Had I forgotten to eat all day again? Damn, I really needed to stop doing that. My body never gave me hunger cues until I was past hungry.

"It's almost ready. Would you set the table, bug?" Dad asked as he flipped the sandwich over, revealing the crispy golden brown of the other side. The trick was homemade garlic butter and a sprinkling of parmesan cheese on the outside. I couldn't *wait* to shove one in my mouth.

"When is Noah getting here?" I asked as I walked over to the dish cabinet, pulling out seven plates and bowls.

"She's working late tonight, so she told us to get started without her," Mom responded.

"That sounds about right," I laughed as I carried the dishes out of the kitchen. Noah was 100% a workaholic, and we had all tried getting on her about having a better work-life balance for years now. But having a work-life balance in the medical field was practically unheard of.

We were twins, but Noah had graduated high school a year before me, having skipped a grade in elementary school. She was autistic and incredibly smart. Very much the overachieving eldest daughter syndrome. She'd also completed her undergrad in just three years, and was in her last year of residency at twenty-six.

I finished setting the round dining room table, and headed back for the silverware we only ever used for family dinner night. Growing up, we'd had a very casual approach to dinner, usually eating in the living room while watching something together as a family. With an ADHD mother, autistic father, and a litter of neurodivergent children, chaotic routines were the norm in our house.

"Come get your drinks, delinquents!" I yelled out to the living room, and was met with a chorus of rebuttals, the loudest from Robyn. Heading back into the kitchen to get my own glass of water, I took the dish piled with the sandwiches Dad pulled from the oven where they had been keeping warm while he made all seven.

Once we were all settled at the table, one chair left open for Noah, we descended into the familiar madness of our very loud family dinners, multiple conversations happening over one another. I didn't really contribute, content to quietly eat my food, basking in the familiarity of it all.

Not long after, Noah entered the house with a shouted, "Honey, I'm home!" She skipped greeting everyone individually and dove right into eating, tearing into her food and stuffing her face. My guess was she hadn't eaten since before her shift. The conversations all ended when Mom let out a piercing whistle to get our attention, Dad and Ezra both cringing at the loud noise.

"You know the drill," she said once she had our attention. Robyn and Alex both groaned. "Time for Highs and Lows!"

Highs and Lows was a thing we'd been doing my entire life, something Mom grew up doing with her family. It was pretty self-explanatory—everyone said their highest point of the day, and their lowest.

"I'll get us started." She smiled brightly, looking around at everyone. "My high today is of course having all my lovely children in the same room enjoying a meal together!" She beamed at us, gripping Dad's hand on the table between them.

They said they got a round dining room table because they didn't believe in hierarchy, but I was pretty sure it was just so they could be touching each other during the meal rather than sitting at opposite ends of the table. They were disgustingly in love, always wanting to be touching each other in some way. It was both sweet and nauseating, but they had definitely set the all of our standards high for future romantic partners.

"And hmm... my low for the day would be that my plant is starting to die again." All of the siblings snickered at that. Mom wished desperately to be a plant person, but every plant she brought home died not long after. She kept trying though, nothing if not persistent and stubborn, despite her black thumb. Dad lifted her hand, giving it a reassuring kiss.

"I'll go next," Ezra volunteered. "My high today was that the restaurant called to let me know the pastry chef will be out of town for a month, and they're having me fill in!" We all issued our congratulations. "My low would be that it's only a month."

Ezra was only twenty-three, which was young even for a sous chef, but he'd started pastry school in night classes during his senior year of high school. Baking had been an obsession of his since he was old enough to talk and asked our mom to teach him how to bake his favorite cookies. There had been no looking back since that first moment.

"Well, my high is the same as your mother's," Dad chimed in, eyes crinkling in the corners. "My low is..." he trailed off, contemplating his answer. "Hmm. It's been a good day so I don't think I have one. Alex?"

Alex actually brightened before speaking. "Actually, today I got an exciting audition for a new sitcom pilot!"

"We're so proud of you!"

"Alex, that's amazing!"

"Someone wants *you* as the lead of a sitcom?"

"Robyn, be nice."

"It's OK, she's just jealous I'm the hot sibling." Alex smirked, and she flipped him off.

"Robyn!"

"You still live under our roof, young lady."

Robyn and Alex both burst into laughter at the simultaneous scolding from our parents, who in turn rolled their eyes at each other. Robyn and Alex bickered like they hated each other, but they were almost as close as Nikki and I.

"Anyways, my low for the day is that I didn't get that cameo I auditioned for last week. But honestly, I'm more excited about this sitcom anyways, so I'm not too bummed." Alex shrugged.

No one volunteered to go next. Robyn was pushing her food around her plate, avoiding participation as usual, and Noah was still stuffing her face like she hadn't eaten in days. "Guess I'll go next, then." I sighed, trying to come up with what to say. "My high is also family dinner—"

"Cheater! You're just copying them," Alex nodded his head at our parents, and I stuck my tongue out at him. He returned the gesture.

"Hey, I haven't been to family dinner in weeks, it's valid. Anyways, before I was so rudely interrupted"—I threw Alex a glare—"I was going to say that my low is that I'm still struggling with my draft. Couldn't get any new words down today."

"Oh, sweetie, I'm so sorry," Mom chipped in, her brows scrunched in sympathy.

"Is there anything we can do to help, bug?" Dad asked. They knew I wrote romance, but thank god neither of them were big readers and they'd never read one of my books. I don't think I could ever look them in the face again if they did. I'd told them I was struggling with my writing, but they didn't know why or what I was struggling with, and I planned on keeping it that way.

"Don't worry, she's getting help from someone already." Noah waggled her eyebrows at me from over her wine glass, and I widened my eyes at her, warning without words that she better be careful what she said.

"Oh, that's great, sweetie, who's helping you?" Mom asked.

"It's just one of my roommates, helping me work through some kinks." Noah choked on the sip of wine she'd just taken. "What about you, Noah? High and low?" I leaned back in my chair, crossing my arms over my chest.

Noah wiped off the wine that had dribbled down her chin, mouthing, *Careful.* I knew she wouldn't actually go all the way there and tell our entire family over dinner what James and I were doing. But she had a viciously competitive streak in her I knew I didn't want to test.

"My high was a really great appointment with one of my little guys who's been struggling. My low was that it was a very long day, and I am ready to sleep for the next twenty-four hours."

We all turned to Robyn, waiting for hers.

"My high is that English class was easy, and my low is that math class was the worst."

A myriad of conversations restarted as we finished up our meal. It wasn't much longer before we had finished up, helping our parents with the dishes before making our respective ways home.

Noah and I walked out to the car together after saying our goodbyes, elbows linked. "Soooo…" Noah started.

"We didn't have sex," I blurted out. Noah raised her brow at me in question. "At least, not yet." And then I told her everything about my first encounter with James, and that we were meeting again tomorrow for our first real lesson.

She didn't say a word at first, just stopping and pulling me close and squeezing tight. Our heads rested on each other's shoulders, and I closed my eyes, relaxing in my sister's arms.

"I'm so proud of you," Noah whispered in my ear.

I didn't know why, but I began to tear up at her words, sniffing loudly against the chilled nighttime air. "Why?" I asked, rubbing my nose along the sleeve of my jacket.

"For asking for what you want, and telling him what you need," she replied. "I know how hard that is for you, so I'm proud of you." God, I was so lucky to have her.

"OK," I said, sniffing one last time. "Enough sappy shit. You know I'm an emotional bitch." We laughed, and I pulled her into one last hug.

"Yes, but you're *my* emotional bitch." Noah placed a smacking kiss on my forehead before I could shove her off. "Now, go get some dick!" she yelled.

I shushed her through my laughter, my face on fire. "You ridiculous nuisance!

Noah ignored me, cackling evilly as she walked to her car, "You know you love me!"

"Unfortunately!" I called back, but I couldn't get the smile off my face as I got into my own car and drove home.

18

James

BE - HOZIER

THIS TIME, WHEN NIKKI opened her bedroom door, she wore only a robe and a blush. I took her in and let out a low whistle. "Look who got undressed up for little old me."

She pretended to slam the door in my face, but I still caught the blush rising up under those freckles. I halted the door with the palm of my hand, "OK, OK, I promise I won't tease you—unless you ask me too." I winked, and this time she couldn't fight the smile forming on her lips.

"Fine, but only because I've been thinking about this all day and the anticipation has me so horny I think I might die."

My cock twitched at her words, and I bit my tongue to hold myself back from saying too much and scaring her off. Nikki opened the door wider to let me in. Her eyes swept over my body as well as I walked past her, taking in my black T-shirt and gray sweatpants, and I could have sworn they lingered on the bulge between my legs.

She shut the door behind me, turning and leaning against it to watch me as I walked over to her desk chair.

"So," I began, "I've been thinking about where we should start." She squirmed where she stood, and my cock hardened even further. My voice grew deeper as I continued, "I know we said we would start with hands, but before we get into any active touching, I think it's best I learn what you like."

She chewed on her lip, a slight furrow to her brow. "You want me to just tell you how I like to be touched?"

"No." I shook my head slowly, a grin spreading across my face. "I want you to show me."

Even across the room, I could see how hard she swallowed, pupils dilating at my words. Nikki was turning out to be much kinkier than I originally thought. "You like that idea, don't you? Me watching you?"

She caught her lip between her teeth, nodding shyly. My smile turned a little serious. "We're staying pretty tame kink-wise, but we should still have a safe word. We both need to know that the other will stop immediately for any reason."

Nikki nodded her head in agreement and walked over to me to sit on the edge of her bed facing me, hands folded in her lap, twisting and wringing her fingers around each other in a stim I'd seen her do often. I hadn't really known much about neurodiversity until I moved in here with her and Collins, but by this point, recognizing the tells and patterns was almost second nature to me.

Smirking at me, she suggested, "Coffee?"

I burst out laughing, nodding my head in agreement, "Coffee it is." I settled back into the chair, one elbow up and resting on the back, legs spread. "Now strip for me," I demanded.

Her eyes flared, chest moving up and down more rapidly than before, but she did as she was told, pulling the string of her robe and letting it flutter open to reveal what was underneath.

She was wearing an icy-blue lace set, the same color as her eyes, and my mouth flooded with saliva at the sight. "Fucking stunning," I murmured, eyes roaming all over her body on display for me. The blue of the lace bra and panties complimented her creamy, pink-tinted skin beautifully. Her black hair cascaded around her shoulders, the flush on her cheeks spreading down to her chest, just brushing the tops of her breasts.

Her belly was rounded, folding over her hips, her thighs large and smooth, no gap between them. Stretch marks decorated her body, scattered across her belly, the inside of her thighs, the tops of her breasts, and where her biceps met her armpits.

As I looked my fill, Nikki pushed the shoulders of the robe down, letting it fall to the ground. She shuffled awkwardly for a moment before seeming to steel herself and straightened, pushing her shoulders back and holding her head high, letting me look my fill.

"That's my girl." My voice rumbled out of my chest like gravel, and I could have sworn I heard the barest whimper fall from Nikki's lips as she rubbed her thighs together, seeking the pressure I knew she needed. "Lay back on the bed," I instructed, leaning my elbows on my spread knees.

She obeyed immediately, sitting on the edge of the bed and lying all the way back until she was staring at the ceiling. "Ah, ah, ah," I scolded. "I need your eyes, NikNak."

"I don't think I can look at you while I do this." Her voice was hesitant, like she was worried I would be upset with her.

"Good girl." Her body jolted with surprise at my words. "I need you to tell me what your limits are. Now I know. Lift your legs for me, darling, and plant your feet on the bed." Nikki hesitated for only a moment before doing as she was told. Spreading her legs, she scooched back until she could plant her feet on the bed, her lace covered pussy perfectly framed by those lush thighs.

I groaned at the sight, the curls covering her pussy just visible through the damp lace. "What now?" she asked, her voice breathy in anticipation.

"Now you take those panties off and touch yourself how you wish I was touching you," I growled, my fists clenched on my knees to keep myself from reaching out and touching her. Fuck, did I want to touch her.

Nikki lifted her ass, dragging the panties down her thick thighs. She flung them to the floor, and I finally got to see what I had been dying for.

Her pussy was fat and covered in a thin layer of dark curls. She used one hand to part her lips, revealing her wet, pink heat to me, and I moaned at the sight. Holding herself open with her left hand, she got to work with her right. She didn't take it slow and tease herself—no, she went straight to her clit, rubbing firm circles around the bud, closer and closer with each rotation, spreading her wetness until her fingers were slick with it. I pressed a hand against my throbbing dick, anything to ease the ache.

She was breathing hard enough for me to hear each inhale and exhale at this point and to see how her breasts rose just over the dome of her stomach, especially on each inhale. Finally, her fingers rubbed directly over her clit, and her back arched up off the bed, her toes curling into the sheets. Her fingers turned frenzied, moving so fast they were almost a blur. Fuck, she was already on the edge, her legs shaking as her body jerked on the bed.

One more moment and she cried out as she fell, her body seizing up in pleasure before crashing back down the bed. Her pants echoed in the silence of the room as she came down from her high. I was so hard by this point it was painful, my cock leaking enough pre-cum to soak a spot through the fabric of my sweats.

Nikki's heels slid off the bed, thumping to the floor. She laid like that for a moment before slowly lifting herself up on her elbows to look at me. Her eyes were glassy with that post-coming pleasure—until she looked down to see just how badly I was tenting my sweats. Then her eyes blazed with hunger as she licked her lips.

Her voice raw with need. "Your turn."

19

NIKKI

I WATCHED AS JAMES swallowed hard, and it made me feel bold, powerful.

"You want me to touch my cock for you, darling?"

"Yes." The word came out on a sigh, my eyes locked on his impressive bulge. "I show you mine, you show me yours, right?"

I swear it looked like he was about to come right then.

"Fuck yes," he breathed the words, already standing up and reaching back to pull the T-shirt over his head. He tossed it to the ground and shucked his sweats next until he stood in front of me wearing nothing but his boxers.

His thighs weren't quite as large as mine, but almost. His chest was soft, his pecs slightly rounded, jiggling with his movements. His stomach was rounded as well, pushing just over the waistband of his boxers.

James slid his hand along the length of his dick, straining against the fabric of his boxers, and briefly squeezed the head. He finally pulled the underwear down, his dick springing free to slap against his stomach, and my mouth went dry.

The head was red and swollen, dripping pre-cum down the shaft, which he used to pull down and lubricate his dick. Grabbing the base, he squeezed firmly, groaning at his own touch. He sat back down in the chair, spreading his legs until I could see his balls, tensed up beneath his dick. I licked my lips at the sight, and he groaned again, "Fuck, Nikki, I'm gonna come right now if you keep looking at me like that."

"Like what?"

"Like you want to eat me," he growled, stroking up his dick slowly. His stared at me through lidded eyes as his strokes started getting faster and faster, his hand twisting on each one. I could feel myself getting wet again from watching him, and I let my legs fall open, my hand traveling down my stomach to where I ached most. I think I enjoyed watching him just as much as I enjoyed him watching me.

"Mmm, you like it when I talk to you, huh?" his voice rumbled as he continued stroking himself, squeezing the head.

A small laugh huffed out of me as my clit throbbed at his words. "I didn't think I would, but fuck, I really do." I began rubbing my clit again as I spoke, the words coming out of me in a whine.

"Fuck, darling, I'm already close," James panted. I could hear the slick sounds of his hand over his dick, and I watched as he reached his other hand down to squeeze his balls.

My fingers moved faster at the sight. "Me too," I cried out. It only took another few strokes before James finally reached his peak, groaning as he came in spurts all over his stomach.

Watching him come sent off my own orgasm, my body locking in pleasure once again as my back arched off the bed. We stared at each other, panting through our come-downs. Had I really just masturbated in front of someone? In front of *James*? Twice?

I don't think I'd ever been that bold before in my life. But the more I thought about it, the more it made sense. Demisexuality was such a nuanced experience, and so many people got it wrong. They couldn't understand our sexual attraction and libido were two separate things. And sure, I hadn't felt sexual attraction for many people in my life yet, but that didn't mean I didn't feel desire, horniness—whatever you wanted to call it.

But here with James, someone I trusted and felt safe with, touching myself to the idea of being touched was a safe way for me to explore that desire. A way for me to get more comfortable with him before we actually touched each other.

As someone who wasn't good with casual intimate touches, I could go weeks without being touched by another human being without even realizing it. All of these thoughts were swirling around in my head, faster than I could keep a hold of, and all at once that post orgasm release of tension hit me, and my eyes started watering.

Why did I always let myself get so touch-starved without even realizing it?

I sat up, turning away from James so he couldn't see the tears sliding down my cheeks. I picked my underwear back up and slid them over my hips. He didn't say anything at first, but I could feel his eyes on me. I heard the sounds of tissue wiping along skin, probably cleaning himself up, and then the sound of him sliding his clothes back on behind me.

"Nikki?" His voice was quiet, unsure from behind me. "What's wrong?"

I sniffed, rummaging in my closet for the softest T-shirt I could find, feeling too exposed and raw. "It's fine," I mumbled, keeping my voice as steady as possible—but I don't think I was very successful.

"Nikki," he said softly, like he was talking to a scared animal he was trying not to frighten. "We promised we would be honest with each other. I need you to tell me about the bad along with the good."

I pulled the T-shirt over my head, pulling up the hem to wipe my tears before turning back around to James, who stood in front of me shirtless, but with his sweats back on.

I looked up to meet his eyes, my heart sending a pang at the quiet look of pain on his face. I tried to wrangle my thoughts into some kind of order he could follow. "It's just... I promise, it was good. It was so good, but afterwards, it felt like a crash and I was just so overwhelmed, and I realized how long it had been since someone outside my family had actually touched me, not sexually, but just at all, and—"

A look of understanding crossed his face, and he interrupted my spiral, "I get it." He raised his hands like he was going to touch me, but dropped it. "It can be a lot of feelings all at once, and sometimes the comedown can be overwhelming."

I took a deep breath. "Will you... will you hold me?"

"Of course," he breathed the words, grabbing my hand and pulling me towards the bed. I followed beside him, stopping just to remove my bra from under my shirt before climbing in after him. I laid facing him, head angled down to the light sprinkling of hair on his chest rather than making eye contact.

Seeming to sense that I was too overwhelmed for face-to-face interaction, James asked quietly, "Do you want to turn around?" I nodded, relieved, and turned until my back was against his warm chest. I tucked my hands under my face between the pillow, and James draped his arm over my waist. Pulling me in tightly against him, he splayed his hand across my stomach under my shirt, our legs intertwining.

For the first time all night, I felt my mind slow to a bearable level. My breathing evened out, the soothing circles he traced on my stomach giving me that pleasant buzzing sensation in my brain, like scratching an itch you hadn't been able to reach all day. I sighed, sinking into the sensation, sinking into him, enjoying the weight of his arm and the heat of his body pressed to mine.

"Will you stay with me?" I murmured. "At least until I fall asleep?"

"Of course."

I drifted into that liminal space between awake and sleeping, but I felt him plant a kiss to my shoulder, that buzzing sensation growing as I began drifting to sleep.

I swear I thought I heard him say something else, but I was already too far gone to know what the words were.

It was the best sleep I'd had in weeks.

20

James

"—AND *THEN*, WARREN BURNT the fucking garlic bread, so there was literally nothing good to eat for the whole meal, and— Hello? Earth to James?" Collins waved his hand in front of my face, and my eyes snapped to attention, realizing I had drifted off again.

"Sorry." I shook my head, refocusing on Collins, who was sitting across the table from me at our favorite Mexican restaurant, telling me about the dinner his coworker Warren had fucked up on his last shift. Pepe's Finest Mexican Dining in La Habra was a fast food Mexican-style diner, and it had the best carnitas I'd ever had the pleasure of eating. I picked up my taco, taking another bite and moaning as the flavors flooded my mouth.

"I promif, I'm lifening," I said through the food in my mouth, and Collins threw a wadded-up napkin at my face.

"Ass. Don't speak with your mouth full."

I washed the food down with a sip of Coke before grinning at him and taking another bite. In truth, I could barely concentrate on anything today. Last night, Nikki had fallen asleep in my arms, and I couldn't stop thinking about it. About *her*.

She'd looked so vulnerable last night, turning to me with tears in her red rimmed eyes. I thought I'd done something wrong, pushed her too far somehow. The relief I felt when she told me what it really was almost had me passing out. I didn't think I could live with myself if I ever hurt her.

Cuddling her had been the best and worst idea. She had needed the human touch, and holding her in my arms had felt better than anything ever had in my life. Better than sex, better than anything. But it had gutted me knowing she didn't feel the same. She just needed *any* human contact in that moment, not that she needed *me* specifically. We hadn't even touched each other yet beyond kissing, and I was already in way too deep.

"Alright." I forced myself to stop thinking about Nikki and give Collins my full attention. "Sorry, I'm with you now. Tell me about Warren fucking up the garlic bread."

"Really, you good, bro?" Collins raised a brow at me, putting his taco back down. "You've been all... spacey to-day."

"Yeah, I just didn't sleep well," I replied, not looking at him.

"Ahhh, I get it," Collins replied slyly.

"Get what?" I looked up at him, brows scrunched.

"You 'didn't sleep well.'" He made air quotes with his fingers, smirking at me.

"Dude, I was home all night. I'm telling you, I just didn't sleep well. That's it." *Yeah, because you were up all night thinking about Nikki.* I told my brain to shut up. "And you? How was your date last night?"

Collins's smirk dropped. "Eh, it was fine."

"What happened?"

"Nothing really. I mean, we hooked up." He shrugged.

"But?"

He shrugged again, taking another bite of his taco and averting his eyes.

"Collins?" He didn't usually shy away from discussing his hook-ups. "You know you can tell me anything, man."

Collins sighed. "I wasn't just looking for a hookup, you know? I feel like I'm finally at the point where I want a real relationship." He shook his head, taking another bite before continuing. "But she didn't want that I guess. Right after we hooked up, she was done with me."

"I'm sorry."

"It's fine. It's not like I *liked* her or anything. I mean, shit, it was our first date. It's just…"

"The rejection of it," I supplied, when it seemed like he couldn't finish the words.

Collins nodded, a crestfallen expression on his face. I'd learned a few things about ADHD over the past four years, and this was one of them. Rejection sensitivity dysphoria, it was called. I'd seen it in both Collins and Nikki. Even though he had only gone on one date with whoever this person was, their rejection of him still stung more than he'd ever really want to admit. It didn't matter who it was, or what the perceived rejection was, it hurt just as bad every time.

"I'm sorry, man, really. I get it." And I did, even if it wasn't to the same extent, but I did understand it on some level. The idea of rejection was terrifying, and I avoided it whenever I could by not rocking the boat and just floating through life instead.

"It is what it is," he smiled at me, more genuinely this time. "I'll get over it soon, I always do."

My back was fucking killing me, and I did not want to be here anymore. I was only halfway through my shift, but it already felt like the longest night ever. The bar was way too packed for a random Thursday night in September.

We'd had rowdy college kids in and out all night, harassing the bartenders, starting fights, throwing drinks. I swear, half the night I'd been two seconds from walking out the door. It was days like these that made me question if I really was content with my life as it was. Did I really want to be a bartender forever?

I used to love it. The excitement, the people, the variety in my days. Maybe I was just getting too old for this shit. Rolling my head around on my stiff shoulders, I finished up the drink I was making, forcing a smile back on my face as I turned back around to give it to the waiting customer. They shoved a five dollar bill in the tip jar, and I gave a quick nod in appreciation.

A break in the crowd showed three familiar faces walking towards me, which was the only thing preventing me from throwing down my apron and bolting. I placed my hands on the edge of the bar, leaning forward once they reached me so I could shout over the noise at them. "Finally! I was about to walk out the door and never come back."

"Damn, that kind of night, huh?" Will reached a hand over to bump my fist, and I returned the gesture, greeting Collins the same way. My eyes met Nikki's bright blue ones and a jolt went through my body. She bumped her first against mine, and I tried to ignore the zing that shot right through me the moment her skin touched mine.

"Oh yeah," I sighed, slumping against the bar in front of them. "Remind me why I chose a job where I have to interact with people again? I hate people."

"You know, I wish I could tell you, but it's beyond me as well," Will mused.

"How long you guys staying tonight?" I asked, shaking up one of the drinks. I swear I could see Nikki staring at the tattoo on my forearm exposed up to the elbow by my shoved-up flannel. I made sure to flex a little extra as I shook the drink.

"Sorry, man, can't stay long tonight. My shift starts tomorrow morning," Collins replied.

"Woooow, prioritizing your livelihood over your friendships? I thought I knew you, dude." I shook my head at him as I set their drinks in front of them.

"I know, right?" Will exclaimed. "It's like he doesn't want to be homeless or something."

"Such a fake friend." Nikki nodded along, hmphing at Collins. She took a sip of the drink I had just set down for her, and I watched, spellbound as her eyes closed in pleasure at the taste. I reached down to adjust myself as subtly as possible, thankful for the bar blocking me.

"So rude," Will said, tsking at him.

Collins pointed his finger between the three of us. "Yeah, definitely not liking this ganging up on me."

"Oh, don't worry, we still love you," Nikki reached up to pinch his cheek, but Collins slapped her hand away with a glare.

"Since when do you take James's side?" He narrowed his eyes, looking back and forth between us. My stomach dropped out, positive that he knew something was going on, until I realized there was literally no way he could.

Nikki winked at him, "Somebody jealous?"

Collins sent her a kiss. "Always when it comes to you, babe."

I was not a fan of this feeling building in my chest, so I turned to Will instead. "What about you?"

"Am I also jealous over Nikki?" Will asked, brows furrowed. "Nah. I'm not the jealous type."

"You know what? Never mind, I'm done with you all." I deadpanned, walking away to take the next customer's order as they all shouted apologies at me through their laughter, begging me to come back. I ignored them, flipping the finger over my shoulder instead.

The next few hours passed in a blur, the bar not slowing down until right before last call. The final customer didn't leave untill almost twenty minutes after we were supposed to be closed. Will, Collins, and Nikki had left a few hours ago, early like Collins had said. I'd had to actively not look at Nikki the entire time, and to be honest, I had no idea how successful I'd been.

Closing the door and locking it, I let my forehead thunk against the wood, my shoulders dropping on a sigh.

"You good?" Sasha asked.

"Yeah." I straightened up and headed back to the bar to start cleaning up. It was just Sasha and me closing, which meant I knew at least that clean up wouldn't be too bad. "Just tired."

Sasha hummed in sympathy, patting my back as she walked past, "We'll be out of here soon." I didn't respond, but part of me was beginning to worry I wasn't just tired in the moment, but tired of this job.

We worked in silence for a few moments before she spoke again. "Oh, James, I almost forgot. There's actually something I wanted to talk with you about."

"Yeah? What's up?" I threw the words over my shoulder, wiping at a particularly sticky spot where one of the rowdy college kids had spilled a drink earlier.

"I'm thinking of taking a step back from the bar." Her words came out casual, the clinking of glass behind me telling me she was just restocking behind the bar like she hadn't just dropped a huge bomb on me.

"What? Why?" I tried to make my voice as composed as possible. I didn't need to know any details about her personal life, but I was desperate to know how she could even think of leaving The Sleepy Siren. It had been her baby for years now. "You'd really sell The Sleepy Siren?"

"Oh fuck no." The words came out on a laugh. "This baby is with me till the day I die. I just really wanna spend some more time with Lauren, and I can't do that if I'm always here, stressing about paperwork or hopping on bar when we're short-staffed like tonight."

It was almost too perfect. Maybe, just maybe, this was the solution to all my problems. It was fate: I was getting tired of being so front-facing at the bar, right when Sasha wanted someone to take over as manager. I felt a bit of hope start swelling inside me.

"I'm thinking of hiring someone to be manager, letting me step back and be kind of a silent owner instead. Focus more on that photography side hustle with Lauren." Sasha's wife Lauren owned a fledgling photography business, but it was a passion they both shared.

But once her words fully registered, my heart sank. "Wait," I said, "So let me get this straight: you're wanting to step back and you're going to hire in a new manager to fill your position instead of promoting internally?"

"Yeah, I figured it would be best that way. I know how much you love tending, and you always say you never wanted to do the paperwork side of this thing, so I figured there'd be no way you were interested." Sasha shrugged again, walking past me to grab another crate of bottles. "And no one else here is qualified enough to take over as manager."

"Right," I responded, my voice wooden. I forgot how much of this crisis about my job had been internal. I hadn't told Sasha anything about how I'd been feeling, so of course she wouldn't know.

The words, the ask, were stuck in my throat. I hated myself for not being able to just ask for what I wanted. I'd never wanted to ask for anything as a kid, didn't want to make my mom's life any harder than it was. It was just easier to stay quiet, to be content with what I had rather than rock the already precarious boat.

"I still haven't decided anything for sure though, so please keep this to yourself a little while longer."

"Got it, boss," I responded, saluting her as I did.

For now, I bottled up what I was feeling. A friend has once told me never to quit on a bad day, and today definitely qualified as a bad day. I needed to sit on it, because as much as I would love to move a little further away into the paperwork and less drink making, I wasn't ready to put myself out there in that way yet.

21

NIKKI

Middle of the Night - Loveless

LAST NIGHT BEFORE GOING to bed, I told myself I was *going* to sit down to write first thing in the morning. I knew I needed to. I *wanted* to, even. Yet it was now almost five, I'd been up since noon, and what had I accomplished?

A big fat load of nothing. I'd woken up and opened my phone, telling myself I would scroll for five minutes just to catch up on all my notifications before getting to work. Yet here we were, four hours later, and I was still in bed scrolling. I'd only gotten out of bed to go to the bathroom and then immediately got back in. Then I'd told myself I would watch just one episode of my show before putting my phone down and turning the TV off again.

The worst part was that it wasn't even like I was relaxed while I watched and scrolled. I felt on edge, my chest tight. My brain just kept screaming *you should be writing* over and over again. And yet I couldn't. Which just made me feel even worse.

I spent half the time I'd been sitting here doom scrolling just *thinking* about my book. Thinking about how I needed to write it. Wondering if something was broken inside me and like I'd never be able to write again. Worried that if I *did* write it and publish it by some miracle, it would get shredded online like the last one. That people would hate the book and hate me, so why even bother in the first place?

It wasn't like I had a very large following. Would anyone even care if I didn't finish the series? Maybe I could just delete all my social media and disappear from the bookish world, and no one would even notice or miss my books. I could go back to a job in retail, letting my soul die slowly more and more each day. Selling my soul to capitalist America was better than making myself vulnerable and risk being hurt, right?

Jesus, I was being such a fucking drama queen. The problem with being a self aware person was that you could recognize your harmful behaviors and patterns, but that didn't make them just up and magically disappear. Sometimes I felt like being aware of it was even worse, because I would still do it, but then I'd feel guilty about it, and then I'd spiral even further, in a never-ending cycle of doom.

So that was what it was like in my brain half the time. The other half of the time, I was thinking about James. Thinking about tonight. About how James was *finally* going to touch me.

My sex drive came in ebbs and flows. Sometimes I could go months without even thinking about getting off, months without touching myself. And sometimes I was so horny I masturbated like I was a teenager, getting off multiple times a day, every day, for a week or more. There were some days where no matter how many times I came, I still wasn't satisfied.

That was probably one of the biggest misconceptions about demisexuality. That because we didn't experience sexual attraction as often as allosexual people, we didn't also feel desire as often. And sure, there were demisexual people out there like that, just like there were allosexual people with low sex drives.

I was definitely at a high point in this cycle. I don't think I'd ever been so horny in my life. It had already been like that before we started this weird little adventure, but ever since that first conversation with James where I'd asked him to sleep with me, it had amped up higher than ever before. It was always the build up and anticipation that got me going the most. Knowing I had a plan, lessons to look forward to, amped it up to a whole other level.

I just hoped that tonight, once I experiences what it was like to have James's hands on me, would finally provide me release and the clarity I needed to write this book.

I looked down at my phone, realizing it was already almost six now, and if I wanted to shower and shave in time, I needed to get up now. Knowing what was coming—hopefully both of us—was the only thing that got me up and to the bathroom for my shower.

I STARED AT MYSELF in the mirror, taking in what I was wearing and trying to decide if it was too much. I'd gotten such a rush from our second lesson, seeing the way he'd looked at me in my lingerie set, that our third lesson called for another one.

I knew his favorite color was emerald green, and luckily I loved the way the color looked on me. So I was wearing an emerald green lace set, without the robe this time, impatient to see the look on his face when I opened the door in nothing but my underwear. Sometimes I questioned why I owned so many lingerie sets when no one ever saw them but me—well, at least until now. But there was something that made me feel so powerful and beautiful wearing delicate lace sets on my fat body, even if no one else saw them.

Fat women were told all the time that their bodies weren't dainty and feminine enough. That fat bodies could never be viewed as dainty in the first place, and that femininity would always be just out of reach for them. Buying and wearing lingerie was my own private fuck you to that feeling. And now, seeing the way James looked at me in the sets? It just made me feel all the more powerful.

A knock on my door pulled me out of my thoughts, and I took a deep breath before walking over to open it. I found James on the other side, this time in nothing but his gray boxers. My eyes immediately drifted down to the bulge between his hips, snapping up when I heard him suck in a deep breath. His eyes were roaming over my body, blazing with heat.

"*Fuck*, Nikki." The words came out of him on a groan, and he swept into the room, slamming the door behind him. I backed up as he stalked towards me, making me step backwards until the back of my knees hit the mattress and I fell back onto my hands, already breathing heavily.

Looking up at him through my lashes, I asked, "You like it?"

He tucked a strand of hair behind my ear. "Perfect," he breathed. "Can I touch you, Nikki?"

"Getting right to it then?" I asked, my voice a mix of anticipation and nerves. At the tone of my voice, James's eyes snapped up to mine from where he'd been hungrily staring at my tits.

"No, darling. I'm not asking to touch your pussy, not yet." My core clenched at his words, wetness begging to dampen my panties. "I think we should start today with kissing, exploring each other's bodies with our hands. Warm you up before we get to it. Does that sound good to you?"

I nodded my head, and he tsked at me. "I need your words, NikNak."

"Yes." The word came out much shakier than I intended it to.

"You remember the safe word?" he asked, and I nodded again.

When he raised his brow at me expectantly, I swallowed before answering. "Coffee."

"Good girl." He got onto his knees in front of me and spread my thighs wide to take his place between them.

A shaky sigh escaped my lips. *Fuck*, I liked the praise more than I thought I would. A shaky sigh escaped my lips at the words, and James smirked like he could read my mind. My skin buzzed with anticipation as I waited for his hands on me.

Leaning in, James breathed against my ear, "I'm going to take my time with you, darling, so I need you to be good and let me." I closed my eyes, letting the words wash over me as I nodded my head in acknowledgement.

He pulled back, a wicked gleam in his eyes, and I swallowed hard as he moved his hands to my knees, slowly dragging them in circles up my thighs, watching the movement of his hands on my skin. I was still leaning back on my own hands, following his every movement. When he got to the apex of my thighs, he retreated, and I held back a frustrated whimper, toes curling into the carpet. Bringing his hands back to my knees, he used them for balance as he leaned forward until he could nuzzle his face into my neck.

I pushed forward, planting one hand on his shoulder and diving the other into his soft curls, lightly scraping my nails over his scalp. I felt his body shudder under my palm, relishing in the feeling of bringing someone pleasure. He pressed his mouth to my neck, letting his lips linger in soft kiss after kiss.

Slowly, he opened his mouth against my skin, sucking gently at the juncture where my neck and shoulder met. I tilted my head to the side, granting him better access. James immediately took advantage, sucking, kissing and nibbling up my neck to my ear, where he pulled the lobe into his mouth, biting just enough to sting. I gasped at the sensation, my eyes falling closed as my hand tightened in his hair.

His hands began sliding up my thighs again, fingers sliding under the lace as he squeezed my ass in his hands, pulling me in closer against his body. I let out a small whimper as my aching center met his, giving me only the smallest amount of relief and leaving me wanting more.

His hands continued wandering, sliding up my sides as he kissed his way from one ear and across my jaw to the other side, giving my other ear the same attention. On instinct my hips rolled again, and James pulled away.

"Ah, ah, ah, not yet, greedy girl." A desperate whine escaped my lips before I could stop it, and he chuckled darkly. "I told you I was going to explore your body before I touched you there, and I keep my word."

He put a palm flat on my chest between my breasts, pushing gently until I took the hint, laying back flat on the bed. "Scooch," he demanded, and I obeyed immediately, wriggling my body up the bed until I was laid out fully on it. James followed after me, hovering his body over on mine, holding himself up on one elbow to prevent him from resting his full weight on top of me. He fit himself into the cradle of my hips, and I closed my eyes, pushing my head further back into the bed as his erection pushed into my clit.

I tried rolling further into him, but he snaked one of his hands down to pin my hip to the mattress. "If you insist on disobeying orders, I can stop," he growled into my ear, biting down hard again, and I cried out at the pleasure–pain of it. I shook my head frantically, immediately forcing my hips still.

"That's my girl." He kissed my ear, soothing the sting of his bite. "If you behave, maybe I'll reward you." He rolled his hips into mine, my back arching at the way his dick ground against my clit. But all too soon, he pulled his hips away again, cutting off the feeling.

Then his hand was in my hair, yanking it back, my entire body buzzing with need, waiting with his lips tortuously close to mine until it felt like I would explode with the anticipation of it all.

22

NIKKI

Andante, Andante - Mamma Mia! Here We Go Again

Just when I thought I was going to die if he didn't touch me, his lips *finally* collided with mine. James devoured my mouth, and my entire body shuddered in relief at the release of the built-up tension, lightning zapping through my body as his tongue dove into mouth, curling around my own. The kiss was so deep I felt like he was trying to lick my soul out of my body, and I moaned into the sweet pressure of it.

I kissed him back with everything in me, looping one of my legs over his hip, my hands diving back into his hair again, relishing in the groan that came out of him when I pulled. The hands at my hips began wandering, tracing across my hipbones, my stomach, tracing the lines of my stretch marks, and I felt more desirable than I ever had before.

I'd done a lot of work to get to where I was in my relationship with my body. I still had hard days, where I wished the stretch marks away, wished I was smaller, wished I took up less space, less so because of how I looked, and more to make my life easier in a world that made it so hard for fat people to merely exist.

But as James traced those stretch marks with reverence, they felt like marks of strength and beauty. He pulled away from the kiss, biting my bottom lip between his teeth as he did. He let go of my lip with a pop, and then his mouth was moving again, trailing kisses down towards my breasts. As he mouthed against the lace over one tit, his hand came up to the other, thumb sweeping over the peak until he found my nipple and pinched it.

"Can I take this off you?" he panted the question against my skin.

"Yes," I replied breathily, and he slid his hand down my back until he could unclasp it. I scrambled to push the straps down my arms and fling the bra off.

"Fuck, you're so pretty Nikki," he praised me, eyes devouring me. Honestly, my boobs were the thing I was most insecure about when it came to my body. I loved how they looked in a bra, but when they weren't contained, they were teardrop-shaped, droopy and nowhere near round or perky. Lying on my back, I knew they fell to the sides of my body, parting down the middle of my chest. Hell, even when my boobs were shoved in a bra, they faced opposite directions.

But James looked at me like I was the most magical thing he'd ever seen. He trailed a path of sweet kisses down between them, using his free hand to scoop one of them up, sweeping his thumb back and forth over my nipple, every touch sending a zap down to my clit.

"So soft," he murmured, lowering his head to the other breast, sucking that nipple into his mouth and scraping his teeth gently across the hardened tip. I gasped, back arching, which only succeeded in shoving my tit further into his mouth. "So sweet," he continued, releasing it with a pop. He blew cool air across the wetness his mouth left behind, and I cried out at the sensation.

James kissed his way back up my body, capturing my mouth in another searing kiss before pulling away just far enough to whisper against my lips, "Can I touch you Nikki?" His hand wandered down from my breast, closer to where I was warm and wet and wanting.

"Please," I begged, on edge from so much buildup with no relief where I ached most. James's hand wasted no time traveling back down my body, and then a knuckle was brushing directly over my center, and even muted through the lace, I was so tightly wound that my back arched off the bed.

"So responsive," James whispered into the skin of my neck. And then he sucked, *hard*, at the same time that he pushed the heel of his hand against my clit. I cried out. "You want all our neighbors to hear the sounds you make for me, NikNak?" he asked, nipping at my lip and slipping his fingers under my panties from the side. He trailed his fingers through my wetness, exploring me with his fingers, while I squirmed and whimpered underneath him.

"Can I put my fingers inside you?" he asked, tracing them around my entrance.

"If you don't, I'll cry," I whined, and he huffed a laugh in response.

"Well, we don't want that," he teased. He pushed a finger into me while also briefly but firmly pressing against my clit. I cried out as my core clenched around his finger, and he smirked at me.

"That feel good, Nikki?" I nodded my head as he slowly pulled his finger out and pushed it back in again. "Do you want a second finger?"

"*Please.*"

Pulling out again, he pushed back in with two this time, and curled them up and forwards. My back arched off the bed as he hit a particularly sensitive spot. *Fuck.* Obviously, I knew what the G-spot was, but as a fat person with short arms, I didn't often finger myself since it was too awkward of an angle, so I'd never really gotten a handle on stimulating it myself. But here and now with James, I got what all the fuss was about.

He hummed against my neck as he kissed his way back up to my lips. He devoured my mouth again, his tongue keeping rhythm with his fingers. One of my hands was still buried in his hair, the other holding the wrist of the hand that was inside me. I could feel my orgasm building, my chest tightening, my thighs shaking. It slowly built and dropped, and built, and dropped. Sweat was gathering on my body, and my heart was racing.

But I couldn't get there.

I could feel tears welling up in my own frustration. James didn't stop, murmuring encouragement in my ear, giving no sign that he was frustrated or upset. "I can't, I can't," I cried, so on edge and desperate for release that I was having trouble controlling my emotions.

"It's OK." James slowed his hand, gently brushing the hair back from my face with his other. "It's OK. What do you need? What can I do?"

"I don't know." I turned my face from him, not wanting him to see the tears falling. James fully removed his fingers from me, shushing me and holding me while I tried to get myself together as my body came down from the edge.

"How do you get there the easiest? Sex doesn't always need to be about coming, but if I can help get you there, I want to do that. Do you use toys? Bring one of them out."

I didn't have the capacity to say anything, and James seemed to understand that, patiently waiting for me to make the next move. I reached over to my nightstand, opening the drawer and pulling out my favorite air pulse vibrator.

"Do you want to use it on yourself so you can have it exactly as you need it? Or do you want me to do it?"

"Can you put your fingers back in me while I use it?" The words came out so quiet I wasn't sure if he could hear me. But he just smiled in response, kissing my forehead.

"Whatever you need, NikNak," he replied sweetly, helping me as I shoved my panties down and tossed them on floor. He watched between my legs hungrily as I turned the toy on, situating it between my legs, directly over my oversensitized clit. I cried out, back arching as the pulses sent lightning zapping from my clit through the rest of my body. James waited only a moment before pushing his fingers back inside me, curling them again and making a come–hither motion against my inner walls.

It was just a few more seconds of the combined sensations before I came, and came *hard*, body locked up so tight I couldn't breathe for a moment, which only made it feel like it lasted even longer. My eyes were slammed shut, and my hand fell limply to the mattress. The toy buzzed away next to me as James continued moving his fingers slowly, bringing me back down to earth.

"You are so beautiful when you come, Nikki." My eyes were still closed, but I could hear the reverence in his voice as he whispered to me. I lay there panting as he continued to whisper sweet nothings, his hand brushing gently against my head, scratching through my hair in a sensation that sent the pleasant buzzing back into my mind.

I couldn't remember the last time I felt so relaxed, my brain quieter than it ever was outside of being high. It was only then that I realized this was the first time I'd ever been fully naked in front of him. Surprisingly, but happily, I didn't feel self-conscious at all. He always made me feel so safe and cared for.

When I finally felt like a human again, I opened my eyes back up, seeing that James was simply watching me, a small smile on his face.

"Better?" he asked, the slightest hint of amusement in his voice.

I smiled back sheepishly. "Someday, I'm gonna come with you without crying, I swear."

He laughed as he curled his body into mine. I felt the hardness of his erection at my hip.

A devilish smile grew on my lips, and I used the element of surprise to push him on his back, moving to straddle his thighs on my knees.

"My turn."

23

James

BABYGIRL - MADDIE ZAHM

MY DICK JUMPED AT her words. *Fuck,* how was she so hot all the time? "You... You don't have to worry about that if you don't want to," I replied shakily, even as my dick yelled at me to shut the fuck up.

Her eyes snapped up to mine from where she'd been staring at the erection trying to punch a hole through my sweats. "I really, really want to," she replied, voice sure and steady.

I gulped at the heat in her eyes, letting out a shaky breath. The words rushed out of me, begging for relief. "Then god yes, I want nothing more than to see your hands on my cock." *And your mouth, and your tongue, and your cunt,* my dick supplied, but I ignored that. *Baby steps,* I had to remind myself.

For all her sudden bravado, she looked a little uncertain when her gaze landed back down on my crotch. Her ass was resting on my thighs, but she rose to her knees to kneel over me so she could pull down my boxers until I could kick them off my ankles and onto the floor. My dick snapped out, sticking angrily into the air, curving back slightly towards my stomach.

Nikki leaned forward, bracing herself with one hand on my hip, tracing the other slowly up my thigh and towards my aching cock that twitched as the anticipation built. Finally, her hand reached my dick, and she traced a finger softly up the shaft.

"*Fuck,*" I groaned. I closed my eyes, my head falling back as I let her take her time, exploring my dick with her fingers. It was torture in the best way. Her fingers were soft and warm, and I swear I was more turned on than I had ever been.

I lifted my head back up to beg her to end the teasing and touch me for real. She saw the movement before I could say anything, and I must have looked like I was in serious pain, because her hand stopped, a sheepish smile playing on her lips.

"I'm sorry." She giggled, biting her lip. "To be honest, I've always been so fascinated about a hard dick. What it would feel like." God, this woman just did something to me. Her look turned sultry as she finally, finally wrapped her fingers around the base of my dick, giving a tentative squeeze. "Will you tell me what you like? I want to make this good for you."

I couldn't look at her with my dick in her hand as she asked how to make it good for me without coming on the spot. I could not come five seconds after she touched me. I would not.

OK, James, think something unsexy. Let's try saying the alphabet backwards. Z, y, x... uhhhh. Damn, I was bad at this. At least I hadn't embarrassed myself and exploded yet.

I realized I still hadn't responded to her yet, her eyes flicking over my face, a question in her gaze. "Yes." My voice came out much hoarser than expected. "I'll tell you what to do."

She waited patiently, squeezing her hand around the base of my dick again. "Spit on it," I demanded. Nikki's eyes went wide, pupils swallowing the blue. She licked her lips, squirming on my thighs, and leaned over to spit on my dick. Without waiting for me to say it, she dragged her hand up and down my shaft, spreading the wetness. Circling once over the head, she gathered the pre-cum there, combining with her spit to slick her hand.

"Mmmm, god, that feels so good," I groaned, closing my eyes again as she continued moving her hand on me. "Now close your fist tighter and squeeze my cock like you mean it." I heard her sharp inhale before her hand tightened and continued to move at the same torturously slow pace.

"It feels even better when you twist as you go," I told her. "Especially when you use two hands and twist in opposite directions."

Nikki leaned back until she was fully sitting on me and could use both of her hands. I could feel her wetness against my leg, and I cursed, turned on even more by the fact that she was so turned on doing this for me. She moved up and down in short motions, twisting her hands in opposite directions as she went, back and forth. On each up stroke, she used her top hand to sweep her thumb over the head. I was panting at this point, way too close to coming and helpless to stop the grunts and noises she was bringing out in me.

Like she could read my mind, Nikki stopped.

My eyes snapped open, whining at the loss of contact as she pulled her hands away. I was so hard the head of my cock was almost purple at that point, and I felt like I would spontaneously combust if she didn't finish me soon.

"Why'd you stop?" I asked, only to find a hungry look in her eyes.

She bit her lip, looking down at my dick. "If it's OK with you, can I use my mouth?"

Is it OK *with me?* "Fuck yes," I breathed. She grinned devilishly before bringing one hand back down to hold my dick steady at the base. As she got closer, she opened her mouth, holding her tongue out to make contact first. It took every ounce of strength I had not to come on her face in that moment.

I slid one hand into her hair, pulling it up and back out of her face so I could watch. And then her tongue was on me, licking one long strip from base to top on the underside of my dick, before swirling a circle around the head.

"Oh god," I groaned. "I'm so close."

Nikki pulled up again. "Tell me before you come. I don't think I'm ready for you to come in my mouth."

"Of course." I moved my hand to rest on her knee. "I'll tap you, but move quickly because I don't know how long I'll last once you put your mouth on me. When you pull away, jerk my cock hard and fast while I come." She nodding in acknowledgment before going back in.

She didn't hesitate this time. Her warm mouth wrapped around the head of my cock as she squeezed the base tightly. She swirled her tongue once around the head, and that was it. I frantically tapped her knee. She pulled back immediately, squeezing the head of my cock with her lips as it fell out of her lips with a pop.

Her hand moved up and down rapidly as I came, spurting in streams over her hand and my stomach.

Nikki

I LET GO OF James's dick, looking down at the come coating my hand. Honestly, any time I'd watched porn, I'd never understood the appeal of a man coming all over a woman and why some women found it hot. But I felt like I kind of understood it now. At least for me, it wasn't the cum itself, but how empowering it felt to bring someone to such immense pleasure.

I was glad he didn't seem upset that I didn't want him to come in my mouth. It wasn't that I wouldn't *ever* be open to trying it, but with my sensory issues including both texture and taste, I had no idea how I would react to it the first time, and didn't particularly want to experiment with it tonight. Leaning over James, I reached for the tissues on my bedside table to clean us up.

As I slid forward, my center dragged across his thigh, and a hiss escaped me.

"Fuck, Nikki, I can feel your wetness dripping on me," James groaned, grabbing my hips. I leaned back, tissues in hand as I cleaned up the mess we'd made of each other. "Do you want more? I'm fucking dying to taste you. And it seems only fair to return the favor." He winked at me, gripping my hips to slide my pussy along his thigh again.

My core clenched, obviously on board already. He sat up so we were face to face, giving me a brief but deep kiss. Then he flipped us around to lay me on my back and slowly kissing his way down my body, stopping to suck on each of my nipples before continuing lower.

"Spread your legs and plant your feet on the bed for me, darling," he murmured against my lower stomach, tracing my skin with his tongue. I didn't realize just how sensitive that area was, but it felt so good. I sighed, melting against his touch as I did as he asked.

He looked up at me as he parted my lips with his hands, blowing cold air across my warm cunt before starting. I gasped at the sensation. He held eye contact while he said, "Hold on, darling." I slid my hand into his curls, clenching in anticipation.

Then that man went to *town*.

My thighs clamped around his head on instinct as lightning sang through my body, and I felt him moan against me as he sucked my clit into his mouth, laving his tongue against the sensitive bud. I had read hundreds of romance books describing this feeling in hundreds of ways, but even as a writer, I didn't think I could ever put into words exactly what it felt like.

My hands tightened in James's hair as he lightly scraped my clit with his teeth. "Oh god," I whimpered, my toes curling into the sheets. Licking down from my clit, he circled his tongue around my entrance. His nose brushed against my clit with every movement, and my body responded by jerking with every brush.

He kept at it, alternating between circling and running his tongue back up to suck at my clit again. Over and over and over, until I was a sweating, panting mess. His hips rutted against the mattress, seeking his own relief. I guess putting his mouth on me turned him on as much as it had me when I'd done it to him.

I could feel the orgasm building, but I knew it was going to happen again. That I was going to sit on the edge right before the fall, unable to get off.

"James," I whined, and he looked up, keeping the flat of his tongue pressed against my clit as he did. "Toy, please."

This time he did pull away, grinning at me. "There's my girl, asking for what she wants." He reached over to grab the toy from where it had been abandoned on the mattress. Turning it on, he put it against my clit, going back to work with his mouth.

And then without warning, I was coming so hard I saw stars, body shaking and seizing.

James pulled his tongue out of me, licking slowly up my slit as I came down. After a moment, once I'd caught my breath, he had pulled back, lifting himself up off the bed. There was a wet spot on the blankets below him where his dick had been.

He looked up at me with a guilty smile. "I'm sorry, I seem to have enjoyed that a little too much."

A warm feeling I didn't recognize bloomed in my chest at the realization that pleasuring me was enough to make him come a second time. "Not gonna lie, that's pretty hot."

24

James

DRESS - TAYLOR SWIFT

SHAKING THE DRINK IN my hands, I poured it out for the customer in front of me, handing it over with a wink. It had been three days since my last lesson with Nikki, and I'd been walking on cloud nine ever since. It was honestly a little concerning. How I thought about her twenty-four seven. The way she smelled, the way she tasted, the way her skin felt under my fingertips, my tongue.

How much I couldn't wait to properly fuck her.

We hadn't had time alone since then, but when we were in the apartment with Will and Collins, it felt impossible not to touch her or even look at her the way I wanted to.

Sitting on the couch watching a movie and wishing I could put an arm around her shoulder and pull her in close to me. Passing her in the kitchen, wishing I could place a hand on her waist. Going to our separate bedrooms each night, wishing I could wake up in the morning, holding her in my arms.

It wasn't real, but god, I wanted it to be. But I knew what this was going in, and just because my feelings for her were growing stronger didn't mean she had changed her mind about me. If all she wanted me for was the lessons, I would take it.

Forcing myself to stop thinking about Nikki at work, I got back to slinging drinks until it was break time, and I could head to the back office. When I opened the door, Sasha was sitting at her desk next to mine.

"What's up, boss-a-roni?"

She rolled her eyes at me. "You know I hate that."

Instead of responding, I blew her a kiss, flopping into my chair and pulling my phone out to doom scroll my fifteen-minute break away.

A few minutes passed in silence before she turned to me. "Oh, by the way, I thought more about if I wanted to step back and hire a manager, and I've decided that's definitely what I'm going to do. I'd love to have your help going through applications with me once it's time to hire." She went back to typing whatever it was she'd been working on.

I froze, taking in her words. It was time to make a decision. I used to think I was perfectly fine where I was, that I didn't want more than this. But I was beginning to understand just how much I needed a change at work. I always tried to be happy and easygoing, but I was sick of staying quiet for fear of rocking the boat. Sick of being afraid to ask for more. And now was the time, before it was too late and Sasha hired someone else.

"Actually, I wanted to talk to you about that," I clicked my phone off, shoving it back in my pocket, and turning towards her.

She stopped what she was doing, no doubt hearing the serious tone of my voice. "What's up?"

I took a deep breath, telling myself I needed to be brave and ask for what I wanted, just as I'd asked Nikki to do with me. "I've been thinking, and I actually want you to consider me for the position." I held my breath after I was done speaking, waiting to see how she would respond. It's not that I necessarily thought she wouldn't be happy about it; I just had no idea how she *would* respond. And I was so used to going through life never asking for more, I had no idea how to not fear that asking for me would be met with rejection.

Her eyes widened in surprise, but she didn't look upset or anything. "I didn't think you'd be interested? You always say, and I quote, 'fuck paperwork, it's stupid.'"

"Damn, woman, do you always have to remember the things I say?" She threw a wadded up napkin at me, and

I ducked out of the way, laughing. "OK, seriously, though," I let the laughter die out from my voice, so she knew I was taking this seriously. "I've realized recently that maybe I wasn't as happy staying where I am as I thought I was. I've felt kinda stuck for a while now. I think this could be a good change of pace for me. And you know I work hard. I know this bar better than anyone besides you. I think I could do it. No, I *know* I could do it." I straightened in my seat, my words growing more confident.

Sasha appraised me.for a moment. "OK."

I blew out a relieved breath, "OK? You'll let me apply for the job?"

Sasha rolled her eyes. "No, dumbass, I'm offering you the position. But hey, if you would rather apply and go through a full round with other applica—"

"Nope, no, that's good. Yes, of course I accept!" I jumped out of my seat and picked her up in a tight hug. Relief and elation washed through me.

"OK, that's enough of that now." She reached up and patted me on top of my head after pushing me away. I was too happy to do anything other than continue grinning at her. Damn, maybe I should try this "asking for what I want thing" more often.

Sasha immediately got started on training me, and the next five days passed in a blur. We figured if she was ready to step back, and wasn't trying to train a new person from scratch, we might as well power our way through it so Sasha could get right into spending more time with Lauren.

It had been five days of paperwork, computer training, more paperwork, backend learning, and oh, had I mentioned paperwork? But it had also been five days of not being stuck at the bar talking to annoying people and flirting for tips. And honestly? Worth it.

When I had told the roommate group chat that I was going to be manager, they'd responded in a range of support from heartfelt congratulations (Nikki), to confirmation that this still meant free drinks for life (Will), to playful ribbing if I even knew what a manager did (Collins). I'd responded to Nikki and Will, and ignored Collins.

It was Saturday night now, and for the first time in what felt like forever, all four of us were home together. We were in the living room watching a Netflix romcom, shouting encouragement and derision in equal measures at the couple on the screen. It was one of our favorite roommate pastimes.

We were all laughing at the hero inevitably saying something dumb to upset the heroine when my phone buzzed. Lifting my hips from the couch, I reached underneath me to pull it out of my pocket. Out of the corner of my eyes I swore I saw Nikki's eyes on my hips as I did, but when I looked over at her, her eyes were on the screen.

I pulled it out to see Nikki's name, and at first I assumed she was sending the roomie group chat a meme or something. I nearly choked on my own tongue when I opened it and read the private message, just between us.

So, when are you gonna fuck me?

I tried to school my face in case Will or Collins decided to look over at me. Nikki and I were at opposite ends of the couch, the guys between us. There she sat, feet curled up under her, her face carefully blank, he body leaning on the arm of the couch so Will next to her couldn't see her phone screen if he looked away from the TV.

Damn, you could warn a guy next time

But it's more fun to see how you react *smirking emoji*

You suck

Is that a request?

Fuck. Whatever she was trying to do, it was working. As subtly as I could, I picked up the couch pillow wedged between me and the arm, settling it over my lap.

Careful, Nikki

Or what?

Babes, don't threaten me with a good time

Did you just quote Taylor Swift at me?

Ngl, the fact that you knew that was kinda hot

LMAO

Where is this coming from?

(Not that I'm not enjoying it)

You haven't touched me in five days

And I'm horny

Are you not?

Do you not see the pillow I had to put on my lap you she-devil?

cry laughing emoji

When do we have the apartment to ourselves again next?

Great question

> I need to do some mental math on Collins's schedule

I looked up from my phone, hoping it hadn't been too obvious. I honestly had forgotten where I was, only thinking about Nikki. That was happening more and more often lately, and I really needed to be more careful. I was going to end up breaking my own heart, ruining our friendship, or both.

I had no idea what had been happening in the movie, too engrossed in my flirting with Nikki. At the moment the couple was having a fight in the rain. And then the hero grabbed the heroine by the face, kissing her passionately.

There was a sigh from the other end of the couch and I looked over to see Nikki watching the scene with a dreamy look on her face. She must have sensed me looking at her because she glanced over.

"What?" she asked on a laugh.

"You're just cu— funny." I caught myself at the last second. "Big fan of the rain kiss, huh?"

"It's just so romantic!" she exclaimed defensively, crossing her arms over her chest.

"Do you *not* like a kiss in the rain?" Collins turned to me incredulously.

"Dude, come on," Will chipped in. "*Spider-man? The Notebook?* It's literally a classic."

"Hey!" I held my hands up in defense. "I never said I didn't!"

Will shook his head at me. "Mm, mm, mm, mm, mm."

"Damn, why are you coming after Nikki like that?" Collins pretended to glare at me, crossing his arms over his chest.

Nikki copied him, pouting at me. "Yeah, James, why'd you come after me?" She put the slightest emphasis on "come" when she spoke, a teasing glint in her eye, and I sent her a dirty look.

"You're all assholes," I grumbled, sulking into my seat and looking away so the guys didn't see the grin I couldn't hide.

Remembering that I was supposed to be figuring out when Collins would be on shift, I did some mental calculations. The next time he went back on shift was October first and second. A few episodes of our favorite reality dating show, and a few sneaky questions later, and I got it out of Will that he'd be covering a game late on the second. I pulled out my phone and shot Nikki a text.

October 2nd. You, me, this dick, that pussy

You're a fucking dork *cry laughing emoji*

Emphasis on the fucking *winking emoji*

25

NIKKI

TALK TOO MUCH - RENEÉ RAPP

I STARED AT THE blank page in front of me, willing the words to magically appear. It was the same routine as always. I told myself I was going to write. I sat in front of the computer. I stared at the blank pages, fragments of sentences floating in and out of my mind, all of them too slippery to latch onto and form into actual sentences. And then I gave up, pulled my phone to scroll for a five-minute brain break, and was still here, hours later, doing abso–fucking–lutely nothing.

Just type, Nikki. Type anything, anything at all, I pleaded with my own brain. I swear some days, it was like I was just in the passenger seat of my own mind, watching ten squirrels in a jumpsuit attempting to act normal. Pretty sure there was nothing normal about that, or even thoughts of that, if I was being totally honest.

My phone dinged with a text, and I sighed with relief, finally having a real reason to ignore the blank page in front of me. It was the family group chat, starting with a message from my twin.

Noah

> Family dinner night bitches (non derogatory), who's in this week?

Robyn

> Oh let me check my very busy schedule, ok yep I'm free

Noah

> *middle finger emoji*

Ezra

> Sorry, not tonight. I'm working.

> Probably? Trying (and failing) to write at the moment

Alex

> Guess I've got nothing better to do

Noah

You bitches (derogatory)

Hey!! I said most likely yes

Noah

I wasn't calling you a bitch, I was calling THEM little bitches.

Robyn

You didn't say little

Noah

Fine, *you little bitches (derogatory)

Better?

Oh, yes, much.

Alex

You're all insufferable

Ezra

Play nice children

Robyn

That's why you're no one's favorite, you never pick sides

Ezra

Maybe that's why I'm everyone's favorite

Alex

> Yeah, he's definitely the least annoying of any of
> us

True

Robyn

> Rude, but not wrong

Noah

> Fine, I'll concede

Ezra

> *gif of someone bowing*

Alright fam, back to work. Wish me luck *salute emoji*

I clicked my phone off and woke the laptop screen up to stare at the blank page again, contemplating if I should just quit instead and go run off to live as a gremlin in the forest. I closed my eyes, taking a breath and forcing myself to chill out. I had a tendency to want to quit when things got hard or I got bored. Writing was the only passion or hobby I hadn't given up on, and I was determined to see it through. I wasn't bored of it in the slightest, but it was definitely the hardest thing I'd ever done.

I was gonna finish this damn book if it killed me.

GETTING OUT OF THE car, I made my way to my parents'
front door, letting myself in. I'd lost track of time and was
running late, so I was sure they'd already sat down to eat.

In the end, I only ended up writing about a page's worth
the whole day. But it was also the first writing I'd done in
months, so I was calling it a win. It was also the perfect
excuse for my tardiness, though in truth I was late because
after I wrapped up writing, I sat down to catch up on
notifications for "ten minutes" that turned into sixty.

"Sorry, sorry! I'm here!" I called out, heading straight for
the dining room. My family was indeed already seated
around the table, digging into dinner. I was met with a
chorus of greetings as I settled into the last open chair.
Tonight it looked like it was homemade alfredo and chick-
en, with a side of garlic bread.

I loaded up my plate, not realizing how hungry I was
until I had the food in front of me. My stomach growled as
I swirled the first bite of pasta around my fork, moaning
as I swallowed it down.

"Perfect timing!" Mom smiled at me as she passed the
garlic bread down. "We were just about to do Highs and
Lows!"

I nodded in response, my mouth full of pasta.

"I'll go first," she continued. "Today's high was an un-eventful day at work. My low was stubbing my toe on the coffee table, *again*." Mom had terrible spatial awareness, and had been stabbing her toe on that coffee table our entire lives, even though the coffee table hadn't changed spots in all the years we'd lived here.

Dad went next. "My high was getting lunch with Dan." Dan was his best friend, and they tried to get together at least twice a month. It was much easier for him to have his plans scheduled in advance, and having specific scheduled time with people helped him stay in contact so he didn't go too long in between hangouts. "My low is that I've had a headache all day, unfortunately."

We all echoed our sympathies, and then Noah volunteered to go next, both her high and her low having to do with patients at work.

"My turn," I jumped in. "My high is that I wrote a few hundred more words!" Everyone congratulated me, knowing how hard I was struggling to write at the moment. "My low is that it took me all day," I added wryly.

Robyn went next, her low a professor who was pissing her off, and high the new tattoo she'd added to her sleeve.

Last to go was Alex. He didn't usually love Highs and Lows, but today he seemed to barely be holding in his excitement. "Well, I was hoping that everyone would be here for this news, but I'll just have to call Ezra when he's off. I got it. I got the sitcom." He had barely finished getting the words out when chaos unleashed, all of us running around the table to pull him up and give him a giant group hug, everyone shouting over each other in an excited cacophony. The rest of dinner was spent talking about what this could mean for Alex, his low forgotten.

After wrapping up dinner and dishes, Noah and I said our goodbyes and headed out to our cars.

As soon as the front door shut behind us, Noah grabbed my arm. "Twin chat time," was all she said before dragging me to her car. I groaned but didn't fight her. "Twin chat" was what we said growing up when one of us needed to talk, no questions asked, no getting out of it.

Once we got in the car, she turned it on to run the AC. As anyone who had ever lived in SoCal knew, September and October were the hottest months of the year. Noah turned to look at me expectantly. When I didn't say anything, she sighed in exasperation. "Girl, tell me how it went!"

I bit my lip, trying to decide how much I wanted to tell her. Normally, we told each other everything. And I know I had promised her to keep her updated, but something about what James and I were doing just felt like... Well, it felt like it was just for us, and I didn't want to share it with anyone, not even Noah.

I shrugged in an attempt at nonchalance. "It's going really good."

"That's all you're going to give me? 'It's good?'"

"I said *really* good."

Noah gave me a deadpan look. "You know I was all for this, but the fact that you don't want to talk about it makes me nervous," she said, her voice full of concern.

"I don't know, Noah, I'm having a good time! We've been taking it slow, we haven't had penetrative sex yet, we're building up to it. And he is definitely up to the task." I grinned cheekily at her, and she tried and failed to hide her snort of laughter. "I'm just kind of enjoying the ride."

"OK, come on." She laughed.

"Sorry, sorry, I'm done now, promise." I grinned at her.

"But seriously, how long do you plan to keep this going?"

"We... haven't really talked about that," I hedged.

"Nikki."

"What?" I asked.

"You know I love you."

"Oh, here we go." I rolled my eyes to the roof of the car in exasperation.

"I'm just worried about you!" Her voice was defensive, but the undertone of care was there. "I'm worried that this is starting to seem more like a relationship rather than just sex lessons like you claim, and you're going to get hurt."

"I promise, I know what I'm doing." I sounded way more confident about it than I really felt.

"Just be careful, OK? With your heart and his."

"I will," I said, holding up my pinky for her to hook with her own. Internally, though, I scoffed. I might have to worry about myself, but there was no way James's heart was at risk of anything.

26

NIKKI

"Holy fuck, Nikki."

James surged into my room, pulling me into his arms and kissing me with everything he had. This time, when James had knocked on my door, I answered it fully naked, only because I'd wanted to see James's reaction. And it did not disappoint. One of his hands wrapped around the back of my head, and the other gripped my waist so hard I was sure it would leave bruises. I relished that idea. I wanted him to leave a mark on me.

I ran my hands down his chest to his waist, running one across his hard dick through his sweats, and he groaned into my mouth before pulling away.

"You seem to be answering the door with less clothes on every time," James mumbled against my mouth.

I bit his lip playfully. "You don't seem to mind."

He hummed in the affirmative. "I fucking love it." Diving back in again, he slammed the door behind him as he licked into my mouth, tongue tangling with my own for a brief but deep kiss.

"Please let me taste you." He pulled away to breathe the words against my skin, then began kissing his way down my neck to dig his teeth into the juncture where my neck met my shoulder.

"Yes, please," I moaned in response. James soothed the bite with his tongue before pulling away and steering me to sit on the edge of the bed, facing the mirror that was my closet door.

With a wicked gleam in his eyes, James got on his knees in front of me. The breath caught in my throat at the sight before me as he lifted one of my legs to throw over his shoulder.

"Hold on, darling," he demanded. "Be a good girl, and watch the show." And then his mouth was on me, and I couldn't think straight. The anticipation of today alone had already had me soaked, and I'd only gotten wetter since the moment he entered my room.

I watched us in the mirror as he licked a firm ⊠⊠stripe up my pussy. I looked beautiful. Wanton, and powerful. Something about the way I watched my breasts sway with each heave of my chest, my leg thrown over his shoulder, how I was completely naked against his still fully clothed form. The way I couldn't see my pussy, just his head moving between my legs.

All of it was extremely fucking hot.

James laved open-mouthed kisses on my pussy, alternating between using his tongue to circle my clit and thrusting into me with his tongue while brushing my clit with his nose. He remembered what had worked best for me last time, and it seemed that this time he was determined to make me come on his own.

Coming up for air, he replaced his tongue with his thumb, rubbing firm circles directly on my bundle of nerves while my thighs squeezed his head. "You want my fingers, darling?" James asked me while kissing a line up my thigh.

"Please," I gasped.

He needed no further encouragement. "You taste so fucking good," he murmured, blowing a cool stream of air across my pussy before diving back in enthusiastically. This time, he stayed focused on my clit, laying his tongue flat against me and pulsing it in waves. I cried out at the sensation, my body jerking in pleasure. And then he slowly pushed one finger into me, and I clenched up even more, as he pumped it a few times before adding a second finger.

He did that same come-hither motion, but this time, I could feel it working. The motions were in rhythm with his tongue on my clit and I felt myself floating higher and higher towards that sweet oblivion. But just like last time, every time I got close, it fell off again.

I whined in frustration, my thighs shaking, heels scrambling against his back.

"I need— I need—" I panted, not actually sure what I needed in this moment.

"Do you trust me?" James mouthed against me, pulling away just enough to speak, but keeping his fingers moving inside me.

"Yes, please, I just need to come," I cried out.

"Safeword?"

"Coffee."

"Good girl," he praised, and then he was back at it again with that tongue of his. But as he continued to build me back up again, he moved his hands from where they'd been gripping my hips, trailing them up my stomach until they found my tits, so his thumbs could brush over my nipples until they were hardened tips.

And then, just as he pinched my nipples, *hard*, he bit my clit.

I screamed, thighs clamping against his head, body arching off the bed until only my head and shoulders still rested on the mattress. I came so hard my ears were ringing, and I swear I might have blacked out for a minute.

I lay there, catching my breath, coming down from one of the hardest orgasms in my life while James slowly soothed my clit with soft, slow licks until I couldn't take it anymore, pulling his head away by his hair.

"Holy *fuck*, James," I panted a breath in between each word, my heart still beating so hard I was sure you could see it pushing against my chest.

James grinned up at me, the lower half of his face wet with my release. "I've noticed something about you, NikNak," he said, his voice smug. "You like a little pain with your pleasure."

I opened my mouth to object, but then truly thought about it. Shit, I'm pretty sure the smug bastard was right.

"Well, I think we would both have to agree that you're right on that one."

He pressed his smile to my skin in a sweet kiss to my thigh. "Are you ready?" he asked gently, and my heart warming at his obvious care.

I nodded. "Yes." And truly, I was. I was so much more settled than I thought I would be now that the time was here. But really, we'd already had sex multiple times by this point. Heteronormativity wanted us to believe sex was only penetration, but any queer person knew that was bullshit. And what we had been doing already *was* sex. This was just another kind.

James pushed up from his knees to stand in front of me so that his crotch was right at eye level. I ran my hands up his thighs, one hand wrapping around to grab his ass, the other massaging his straining cock through his sweats. He groaned, head falling forward as he brushed a thumb across my cheek.

"Careful, if you want this to actually last," he murmured.

I gave him one last squeeze before pulling my hand away. "Condom?"

He reached his hand in his pocket and held it up between two fingers.

I reached out to grab it, and then hesitated. "Can I put it on?" I asked shyly.

"Want your hands on my dick that bad, huh?" He smirked at me, and I winked back. I put the wrapper in my teeth as I used both hands to pull down his sweats, watching greedily as his dick sprang out. He reached back and pulled his black T-shirt up over his head.

Carefully, I tore the wrapper open and positioned the condom over his dick, using both of my hands to roll it down, then giving him a few strokes just for good measure.

I looked up at him, biting my lip nervously. "I did that right, yeah?" My voice was slightly uncertain, not wanting to ruin the moment, but needing to make sure I was doing everything correctly.

James started down at me hungrily, grabbing my hands and pulling me up. "Yes, NikNak. That was perfect." He kissed me deeply, shoving his tongue in my mouth, grabbing handfuls of my ass and pulling me into him, his dick pushing into my soft stomach.

James pulled back from the kiss just enough to speak against my lips, "Now I want you to turn around, lean over on the bed, and stick that pretty ass in the air for me, darling." He nipped my bottom lip before pulling away and waited for me to obey his command. My clit throbbed at his words, eager and ready for him.

I swallowed down the last of my nerves and did as he directed. Leaning over, I rested my elbows on the bed, turning my head to the side, ass up in the air. Shuffling my feet, I spread my legs further apart until I was fully on display for him.

I couldn't see what he was doing, and the need for his touch set me even more on edge, until I felt like I was dripping with desire. Suddenly I felt his hand smooth across the side of my ass, and I jumped lightly at the touch. Immediately, James pulled his hand back.

"No," I gasped. "Please don't stop. I promise, I remember the safe word, and I'll use it if I need to."

His hand was back on me, a soft word of encouragement from him letting me know he understood. His other hand joined in, both of them now roaming my body, squeezing handfuls of my ass. One hand ventured towards my center, swiping though my wetness, and I moaned at the touch.

"You're so fucking wet for me." The words were followed by the sound of sucking on his finger and his groan. "Fuck, you taste so good." My clit throbbed again, and this time I could definitely feel the wetness dripping down my thighs.

"Now, I'm going to fuck you. I'm going to start slow, but you have to be vocal and tell me what you need. Understand?" He smoothed his hands over my ass again, one lifting to smack sharply against my flesh when I didn't respond right away. I cried out at the mix of pleasure and pain. "*Understand?*"

"Yes!" I cried out, desperate for him to get inside me. One hand left me again, the other sliding up to grip my hip firmly. And then, *finally*, I felt the head of his cock nudging at my entrance. Impatient, I pushed back towards him, the head finally slipping inside and stretching me in the most delicious way.

He stilled where he was, just the tip inside me.

"Needy girl," he admonished, landing another smack on my ass. He cursed as I clenched around him on a moan. "Mmm, you really do like that, don't you?" He smacked the other cheek this time, pushing a little further in at the same time, and I cried out.

Slowly, he began thrusting into me, then drawing back before pushing a little deeper each time, until he was fully seated inside of me. He stilled for a moment, both of us panting. Then he gripped both of my hips tight in his hands, holding me steady as he worked himself in and out, only slowly increasing his speed as he stretched me out around him.

I may not have had sex with any other person before, but I had used plenty of toys on myself, including dildos. I'd always wondered how different it would be with an actual dick. To be honest, it wasn't so different in feeling, though it was warmer, and my arms weren't as tired. He began thrusting faster, pulling my hips back to meet him with every thrust. Once he really started going, giving it some force, I cried out at the new feeling, the sounds of us echoing around my room.

He seemed to be reaching spots inside of me I never could on my own. That was the other thing with using a dildo as a fat person with short arms. You could only reach so far, at so many angles.

From there, I was a moaning, whining mess. Occasionally, he continued to smack my ass in varying degrees, and each time, I cried out, clenching around him.

"I'm close, Nikki," he panted, his rhythm beginning to falter as he lost himself inside me. "Touch yourself, please. Come with me."

Wasting no time, I snaked a hand down under me until I could reach my clit and rub in firm, tight circles. The combination of his cock hitting that one spot inside me while I touched my clit pushed me right up to the edge, my thighs shaking, knees in danger of buckling at the pleasure of it all.

"James!" I cried out. "I'm gonna come."

After a few more frantic thrusts, James stilled inside me. "Fuck!" he roared as he came, his dick throbbing inside of me. That sensation is what finally sent me over the edge. I came around him, his dick inside me as my pussy clenched down on him dragging the orgasm out.

After a moment, James gently pulled out of me, the feeling of it drawing a soft whine from me. He rolled me over into his arms so he could hold me face-to-face and place a gentle kiss on my forehead before guiding me to lay on the mattress.

I watched through half-lidded eyes as he went to dispose of the condom. "I'll be right back," he promised, holding my gaze until I nodded that I had heard him. He came back with a warm, wet cloth, and cleaned up between my legs, tossing it into the dirty hamper. He climbed in bed next to me, spooning me the way he had the first time.

I closed my eyes at the sweet kiss he pressed to the back of my neck. "How do you feel?"

I sighed contentedly, settling into his arms as my eyes drifted closed. "Perfect."

27

James

SAME BOAT - LIZZY MCALPINE

OVER THE NEXT TWO weeks, if I wasn't working and we had the apartment to ourselves, we were fucking. Anywhere and everywhere.

One day, Nikki blew me in the shower and made me come so hard I nearly slipped and brought us both down, out laughter bouncing off the shower walls. I fucked her from behind over the back of the couch while the movie we were watching played on in the background, forgotten. I ate her out on top of the dining table after she asked me what I wanted for dinner one night and I responded, *you*. We made sure to disinfect it thoroughly afterwards.

But it was starting to become more than just sex, at least for me. I fully gave up on denying it to myself any longer. I was in love with Nikki. Fully, madly, deeply in love with her. I tried not to let myself get my hopes up too much that she could feel the same, but sometimes I swore she looked at me differently. Like more than a friend.

Like the other day, when we'd had a rare night of SoCal rain. All four of us had been in our own rooms, and I looked out the window to see the rain coming down. I hoped the guys were already asleep, and I snuck to Nikki's room after texting to see if she was awake. When she opened her door, I held a finger up to my lips, grabbing her hand and dragging her out of the apartment. She followed behind me, confused but giggling all the same. I led her out onto the street until we were standing in the rain, immediately soaked to the bone.

She asked me what I was doing, but before she could finish the sentence, I'd grabbed her by the face, pulling her in for a deep kiss. She reached up and grabbed my wrists, melting into the warmth of my mouth on hers. I'd bitten her lip, pulling away to rest my forehead against hers.

"Another box to check off your list," I whispered.

I saw a look in her eyes that night I'd never seen before. Maybe it was all in my head. Maybe I was delusional for thinking she would ever love me back. But I had to try. And I had an idea.

What are you doing tonight?

I assume you're looking for an answer other than you?

I've created a horny monster

Please, you can't take credit for what I've always been

I concede *cry laughing emoji*

For real, though, why?

I had an idea

I think we should go on a date

A fake date, for research purposes

I have been on dates before you know

Yes, but have any of them been good?

Damn, rude

But unfortunately, also accurate

So?

I don't know...

Do you think this is a good idea?

> I promise I'll be on my best behavior

> *gif of someone making the sign of the cross on their chest*

Ok, I'm in

But you're paying

For the accuracy of the research of course

> *gif of Westley from* The Princess Bride *saying "as you wish"**

Smiling down at my phone, I tried not to let my excitement get the best of me. This was a *fake date.* I had to remember that. The next step was using this fake date to get her to see what it could be like for real, if she wanted it.

I had planning to do.

Nikki

I WAS ONLY SLIGHTLY panicking. I had no idea why James had asked me to go on a date—a *fake* date—with him. And I didn't know how I felt about it. I just kept hearing Noah's words, *be careful*, repeating in my head.

The thing is, a part of me really wanted to go on a date with him. Just to see what it was like. I'd gotten to experience the sexual side of him, but part of me was curious to see the romantic side as well.

But maybe I already had been seeing that side of him, and just hadn't noticed. The night he pulled me outside to kiss me in the rain flashed in my head, the weird feeling I'd gotten in my chest as he looked at me. But just because he remembered something I'd said, and then actually done something about it didn't mean that he actually *liked* me. In all the years I'd known James, he'd never been in a relationship. I didn't know if he even wanted that for himself, or if he was content as he was.

Besides, I could barely take care of myself, barely get through what I was supposed to do when it came to work. I didn't have the capacity to be in a relationship. To give that person the time, and energy they deserved from a partner.

I forced myself to finish getting dressed, and to stop thinking so deeply about it, and reading too much into everything. James knew I needed help getting past this mental block, needed help getting inspired to write again, and he was just trying to help. That was all.

I looked at my watch, realizing I needed to get out the door if I didn't want to be late. James had texted me to meet him at the Cheesecake Factory. It was one of my favorite restaurants, which he knew, but it wasn't some super fancy place that would make this fake date feel all too real.

He'd said he had a few errands to run beforehand, which was why he was having me meet him there, and I was grateful for that. Him driving me there would have made it feel too much like a real date, and I needed to make it clear to my brain that this was just for practice.

When I got to the restaurant, James was waiting outside for me, holding a paper orchid. How did he know that was my favorite flower?

He handed it out to me, my fingers tingling as they brushed his. "I figured a bouquet would be too much." He shoved his hands in his pockets. "And this way, it won't die on you."

It was beautiful. I smiled at him and slid the flower into my purse. "Thanks." He opened the door, letting me walk past him. He went to check with the host to see if our reservation was ready, and I chewed my lip, looking around. I'd never come here on a date before, but I'd of course seen people on dates around me when I went with friends or family, and I'd always thought it was a romantic, if cheesy, place to go on a date. But who didn't love a little cheese sometimes?

He came back with the host who led us to our table. We settled in, and I picked up the menu, pretending to browse like I didn't order the same thing every time. I just needed a minute to get my bearings. I had no idea what to talk about. Which was stupid! We were friends and room-mates, and lately, fuck buddies. In our four years of living together, I had never felt awkward or like I didn't know what to say around him. I knew this date was supposed to be fake, but something *felt* different.

"So, come here often?" His voice floated over from the other side of the menu covering his face.

I snorted. "What are you doing?" I asked.

"Breaking the tension, as I do best." He gave a little self satisfied bow and I laughed again.

"You are such a fucking dork." I shook my head at him, but the huge grin on my face softened the severity of my words.

"Yeah, but I got you laughing, didn't I?" He winked at me, picking up his own menu to browse.

I relaxed into my seat, realizing he was right, and I was much more relaxed now. I was noticing more and more how often he did that for me.

"Alright, I'll play along," I replied. "So, *Josh*, what do you do for work?"

"It's James, actually." He grinned, catching on to my game.

"Ah, yes, James, sorry!"

"No worries. I'm a bartender—the assistant manager at a bar, actually."

"That must be fun."

"It can be," he hedged, nodding his head side to side. "But I just got a promotion to manager so my boss can step back and spend more time with her wife and their photography side hustle."

"Oh, that's incredible, congratulations!"

"Thank you!" His smile was genuine and infectious. "And you? What do you do for work?"

"Oh, you know, I do website copywriting."

James raised a brow and broke character to ask, "Do you usually lie about your job on first dates?"

I shrugged, contemplating my answer. "I haven't been on that many dates, but honestly? With men, most of the time yes. When it's a woman, it's not so bad, but have you *met* men? Can you imagine what they would say to me if I said I write romance?"

James cringed, leaning back in his seat again. "Oof, yeah, OK, forget I asked."

We settled back into our "first date" roles, the conversation flowing from there. It was weird how not-weird it was. Everything was always just so easy with James. Familiar, and comfortable. I never imagined it being like this between us in a romantic way, and I had to keep reminding myself that this was a *fake* date. That I didn't *want* it to be a real date.

By the time dinner was done and we were eating our dessert, it was getting harder to remember that. After paying the bill, James leaned in close, a mischievous look in his eye.

"So, Nikki. You wanna come back to my place?"

I tapped my lips, pretending to think about it. "Well, I've never gone home with someone on a first date before, but I guess there's a first time for everything."

28

NIKKI

BED CHEM - SABRINA CARPENTER

COLLINS WAS ON SHIFT, so when we got home, we checked to make sure Will was also gone. He'd been spending more and more time at the studio, working later hours than he usually did. Once we confirmed the apartment was empty, James pushed me up against the wall outside my bedroom door. Holding me by the chin, he kissed me slow and deep, my toes curling in my shoes as his tongue plunged into my mouth.

I placed a hand on his chest, gently pushing him away. He pulled back, searching my eyes. "Is everything OK?"

"Yes," I assured him with a smile. "Everything is great. I just... there's something I've always wanted to try." I bit my lip, looking down at my hand on his chest. I wasn't sure if he'd be into my request, but he had said he didn't think there was a boundary of his that I could cross, so I might as well at least ask.

He tucked his hand under my chin, lifting my face until I met his eyes. "Anything, NikNak."

"So when I uh, take care of myself"—I knew my face was as red as a tomato, which all things considered was ridiculous I was fully aware—"it's always more pleasurable when I'm high."

His eyes lit with understanding, "Ahhhh, I see where you're going with this. You wanna have sex high, don't you?"

I nodded. "Is that something you'd be into? Have you ever done it before?"

"Yeah, my college boyfriend and I. It was always some of our best sex, actually," He laughed. "You feel safe being inebriated with me while we have sex?"

"I do," I responded immediately. "And you would feel safe with me?"

"Absolutely," he answered without hesitation. "Since it's your first time, we should definitely start slow. How many milligrams do you usually take?"

"For a light buzz? Twenty. When I wanna get high off my ass? Forty."

He raised a brow at me, impressed. "Damn, girl. That's a pretty high tolerance."

"Yeah, it's cool until you realize how expensive weed is."

"Fair point. Well, let's start with fifteen then, yeah?"

I nodded eagerly in agreement, telling him to meet me on the couch and running to grab my edibles. Bringing them back out, I split them between us, settling on the couch next to him.

"What do you want to watch while we wait for it to kick in?" James asked, leaning back into the couch, one hand pointing the remote at the TV as he started it up, the other stretched out across the back of the couch. I leaned into him as he began flipping through our streaming services.

"I would say we should get you to finish up *Is It Cake?* season three, but we have no cake in the house, and with the munchies, I am not doing that to myself."

James threw his head back in laughter. "Yeah, that's probably smart. I'm not sure what I would do with a munchy-hangry Nikki."

"Please, as if you wouldn't be in the exact same boat," I scoffed.

Without taking his eyes off the TV, he leaned in closer and whispered in my ear, "I have something much sweeter I plan on eating tonight." He pulled away again, as if he hadn't just soaked my panties in a handful of words.

If he was going to play dirty, so was I. "Did I mention that the only time I've ever squirted was while high?"

"Fuck," James groaned, head falling back on the couch. "You win. I don't know why I thought I could outdo a romance author."

He rolled his head towards me, grinning, and I cracked up. I fell back against the couch and settled further into his side. "Something we've seen before," I finally answered his original question. "It's not like we're going to finish the full thing."

"Mmm, good point. *Pride and Prejudice?*" he asked.

"They're both so *hot*," we said at the exact same time, turning to look at each other and bursting into laughter.

"God, I love being bi," James sighed as he turned the movie one, settling back into the couch.

"Same."

The movie started, and we relaxed, watching as the hi-jinks of the Bennet family ensued. As time went on, we sank further and further into each other, until I was fully leaning against his side. I kept adjusting how I sat, however, and I felt bad that I was jostling him. I just could never sit in one position for too long before my legs got restless, feeling like they were in pain until I moved positions.

At one point, I had my legs stretched out resting on the coffee table, but that wasn't feeling comfortable either. After the tenth time I readjusted, James turned to me.

"Here," he said, grabbing my legs, and laying them over his thighs, leaving one hand wrapped around my thigh right above my knee. "Better?"

"Much," I sighed.

We continued watching the movie that way, and James's hand stayed where it was. And then he started rubbing it along my leg. Slowly at first, just his thumb sweeping back and forth. Then his entire hand back and forth from the inside of my thigh to the outside. Then it slowly began migrating higher and higher, until it was fidgeting with the hem of my skirt.

The longer it went on, the more turned on I got, and the more I squirmed in my seat. I know he felt me moving against him, and I knew he was just as affected as I was. I shifted my thighs higher up on his lap until I could feel his erection pressing up against the bottom of my thigh. Now every time he made me writhe with his touch, my thigh rubbed against his dick. As we sat there teasing each other, both of us getting more and more riled up, I realized the edible was really starting to kicking in.

The main reason I enjoyed getting high was that it was one of the only ways I could get my brain to go quiet. I was floored when I found out neurotypical people's brains didn't have constant, twenty-four seven noise in their head. Even when I wasn't thinking about something, I was thinking about how I wasn't thinking about anything.

But when I was high, my body usually responded one of three ways. I would pass out quickly, something I was never able to do sober. Or it was a pleasant nothing, a soft buzzy feeling, like my brain was in a vibrating massage chair. Or I got ridiculously horny.

Seeing as I'd already been horny before getting high, it was definitely the latter today. Being high made every sensation of pleasure feel exaggerated. While the rest of my surroundings faded into fuzzy out-of-focus background, my pleasure was even sharper and more present.

I giggled at whatever joke had just been said in the movie and turned to look at James. Only he was already looking at me, his gaze smoldering. A rush of wetness soaked my panties.

Okay, so James also got even hornier when he was high.

"Mmm," I hummed as his hand slipped higher, brushing the outside of my panties. "It's hitting for you, too, isn't it?"

"It is." His voice rumbled out of him, warm like melted honey. He rubbed his fingers more firmly against my seam through the damp fabric. "I see you're already wet for me."

I moaned softly, eyes fluttering closed as my brain floated away into the clouds. "And you're already rock-hard for me."

"You know what I want right now?"

"Hmmm?"

"I want you to sit on my fucking face."

"Fuck yes." I jumped to my feet, swaying slightly and giggling as I caught my balance on his shoulders. While I was leaning over him, I decided his face was too close *not* to kiss and did just that. James straightened in his seat, reaching up to meet me.

He broke away, panting. "Bedroom, now."

He jumped up and grabbed my hand, and dragged me to my room. I pulled back on his arm before he could lay down, going to my closet and pulling out a blanket, throwing it over the bed. He looked at me in question and I felt my face burning, but I couldn't stop my giggled as I explained, "The first time I squirted after masturbating while high, I went online and bought a waterproof blanket. It's so much easier to clean up after."

He looked at me in awe. "Oh shit, that's so smart!" We looked at each other, devolving into laughter again. Once we'd caught our breath, James pulled in me closer, kissing me again. He kissed me like he never wanted to be doing anything else. It was maybe a little sloppy, but it felt so *good*. Like we were floating in a world of our own, just the two of us.

"Now, I'm going to lie on that bed, and you are gonna sit on my face, and I am going to make you come," James ordered as he kissed up the side of my neck, sucking my earlobe into his mouth and biting it before letting go and flopping back onto the bed.

I started to take off my dress, but James stopped me before I could. "No, leave it on. Just take off your panties." I shuddered in pleasure at the command in his voice and obeyed, pulling my underwear off and tossing them to the side.

There was something so *wanton* about fucking while fully clothed, like you couldn't wait one more second to be with each other. I climbed onto the bed, straddling James as I shuffled up his body to his face. Hovering over him, I lowered myself until I was right above his mouth.

James grabbed my hips, and the last thing I heard before his mouth was one me was the command, "I said *sit*." And then he yanked me down until my pussy was fully sitting on his face, and I immediately cried out in pleasure, throwing my head back as I gripped onto the headboard for stability.

Every feeling was magnified, and I felt the ringing pleasure echoing through every bone in my body as his mouth moved against my pussy, licking and sucking and occasionally nipping at my most sensitive places. It was no time as all before I felt myself getting close. I could feel it building in me, feel that extra prick of pleasure that was almost like pain but also better than anything I ever felt, that told me he was going to have me squirting.

And then he added his fingers curling into me, finding that one spot and pressing hard right as he sucked my clit into his mouth and scraped his teeth against the bundle of nerves, and I came so hard I may have blacked out for a second. I could feel the wetness dripping out of me, soaking James's face.

He licked up every last drop.

29

James

BURNING HOUSE - JULIA WOLF

THAT MAY HAVE BEEN the single hottest experience of my life. I also was harder than I ever had been, the combination of the weed and just *Nikki* leaving me feeling desperately feral for her.

She collapsed on the bed next to me, still panting. "Shit, you really do know what you're doing."

"I've practiced a time or two," I joked, and we both laughed again.

She turned on her side, propping her head up on her elbow, trailing her eyes up and down my body. "Well, I need to get in some practice of my own." She stared at me through half-lidded eyes. Suddenly, she lit up. "Omg, I have the best idea! Do you have handcuffs?"

A slow grin, spread across my face. "Yes, I do. You want me to use them on you, or you wanna use them on me?"

"I want to tie you to my bed, and kiss my way across your entire body."

My dick jumped in my pants, my entire body screaming *yes*. "I'll be right back." I scrambled out of the bed and ran to my room. Once I found the handcuffs, I quickly made my way back to Nikki's room. She was walking around the room, lighting a few candles.

Following her lead, I clicked off the light, and she looked up at me, her eyes warm and just a bit hazy. The edibles had definitely fully kicked in by now for both of us, and I felt lighter than air.

I wrapped my arms around her before walking us back to her bed. "I can't wait for you to have your wicked way with me," I told her. I put my hands above my head, grinning while I waited for her to get started. She leaned over me, giving me a quick kiss before reaching up higher to grab my wrists. Her tits were right over my face, so I kissed along the mounds as she handcuffed me around one of the bars of the headboard.

She climbed on the bed, throwing a leg over my waist to straddle me. Leaning down, she hovered her lips above mine, pulling away when I reached my mouth up for her. "Ah, ah, ah," Nikki admonished. "It's my turn to be in change," she whispered the words along my jaw, sighing softly against my skin as she went. "You just lay there and look pretty."

She kissed down my neck, licking and biting as she went. She paused to shove my shirt up under my armpits so she could kiss along my chest, scraping her teeth against each of my nipples. My legs jerked, lightning zapping from my nipples down to my dick.

She slid her body down until she got to my stomach, paying special attention to kissing along my stretch marks as I had done with her. Once she got to the edge of my pants, she popped the button and unzipped them to slide them down and off my thighs before tossing them over her shoulder. Leaving the boxers on so the sensations were muted, she mouthed along the impression of my dick pressing against my boxers.

My eyes fell closed, my head buzzing as the feeling of her lips on me set my entire body tingling.

"Please," I finally gasped.

"Please what?" She smiled lazily at me, then licked a line up my cock.

"Please put your mouth on me. I need it, I need *you*," I begged.

My eyes were hazy with lust and weed, ears ringing with pleasure, and I could swear Nikki was glowing. She pulled my dick out of my boxers, and my eyes closed when she lowered her head to take me in her mouth.

"Fuuuuck," I groaned at the heavenly feeling of her warm, wet mouth enveloping the head of my cock. Her tongue circled around me before sliding down to press against the vein on the underside. She reached one hand down and tugged slightly on my balls, and I opened my eyes, needing to see my cock disappearing further into her mouth as she began taking me in.

That's when I realized I had been wrong earlier. Nikki wasn't glowing. It was her dresser behind her, which was currently on *fire*.

"Oh shit!" I yelped, trying to sit up, only remembering I was handcuffed to the headboard when my wrists were yanked back. "Ow!"

"What? What did I do?" Nikki's eyes were wide with concern.

I gestured behind her with my head. "Fire!"

"What, your dick's on fire? Are you allergic to something?"

"No, there's an actual fire!"

Nikki scrambled around to look at it, cursing, and I could finally see the full thing. When she had thrown my jeans over her shoulder, they had landed on top of one of the candles and gone up in flames.

Smoke was slowly filling the room. Nikki jumped off the bed, running towards the fire before stopping and looking around. She looked back at me, eyes wide. "How do I put out a fire?" she yelled.

I tried to think, but my brain felt too sluggish. "Stop, drop, and roll?"

Nikki laughed. "That's only when *you're* on fire, dumb-ass."

I smiled. "Oh shit, yeah, I think you're right."

"Oh, water!" Nikki ran from the room. I went to get up to help her, forgetting *again* that I was handcuffed. "Shit!" And then for some reason I laughed again. Deep down I knew this was not funny, but my weed-addled brain thought it was fucking hilarious.

"Nikki, where are you?" I yelled. A moment later Nikki came careening around the corner, a giant pot filled with water sloshing on the floor. She threw it on the fire, dampening most but not all of it.

"Damn." She looked back down to the empty pot. "Gotta get more, I'll be back." She ran from the room again, and I lay there uselessly, watching the flames flicker across the dresser. I realized that my ears hadn't been ringing, it had been the fire alarm going off. Nikki raced back into the room, tossing another pot of water onto the dresser again. This time, it took the rest of the flames out, leaving a smoking, blackened dresser and half-incinerated jeans.

Nikki was panting, staring at the dresser, before she burst into laughter as well. "Dude, what the fuck?" She wiped tears of laughter from her eyes. My laughter joined in with hers before we both started coughing from the smoke.

"Damn, I thought my eyes were just hazy from the weed, but I guess it was the smoke." I giggled, trying to sit up and getting yanked back down again.

"Oh yeah." She looked around the room, seeming to notice it for the first time. She opened a window to get the smoke out, and that was when we heard the front door bang open. Our heads whipped around to each other, yelping "Fuck!" at the same time.

Nikki looked around in a circle like she was searching for something.

"What are you looking for?"

"I lost the key!" She slapped her hand over her mouth, her shoulders shaking with laughter. I joined in, arms shaking against the cuffs.

Collins's voice hollered, "Nikki, James! Is anyone home?! Are you guys ok?"

Will's voice came next. "You check Nikki's room, I'll check James's!" followed by thundering footsteps down the hallway. It was only then that I realized my dick was still pressing against my boxers, visible through the damp white fabric.

"Nikki, I need to cover up!" I whispered at her.

"Omg, you're still so hard," she whispered back, throwing a blanket over my lap. "Wait, we need a backstory, what do we tell them?" Nikki looked at me frantically, eyes wide with panic and I couldn't help but think how cute she looked.

"I don't know, you're the writer!" I shot back.

She gasped. "You're right!" But it was too late, because just then, Collins burst through the door.

His shoulders drooped in relief when he spotted us, and he called out, "Will, they're in here!" He continued scanning the room after that, taking in the burnt dresser and half melted jeans, before turning back to us. "Is everyone ok? What the fuck hap—" His eyes scanned over Nikki, who was standing next to the bed and trying to keep herself from laughing, but she couldn't hold back her cute little snorts.

And then his eyes jumped to me, his brows raising as he took in my hands cuffed up above my head and the blanket thrown over my lap with my bare legs sticking out the other side. My chest shaking with silent giggles. "James, are you handcuffed to Nikki's bed frame? What the fuck? Are you two fucking?"

Will burst into the room next and stopped short at the sight of the dresser, then Nikki, then me. "Uhhh, what did we just walk in on?"

Nikki and I looked at each other, bursting into laughter, Nikki's face as red as a tomato.

"OK, explain," Collins said, impatient. "Why the fuck are you handcuffed to Nikki's bed, James?"

"Uhhh..." I looked at Nikki, trying to gauge what she wanted me to say, but she was still covering her mouth trying to stop her laughter.

Collins's eyes flicked between us before a smile grew on his face, "Wait, are you both high right now?" He turned to Will. "They're totally high right now."

Will leaned forward, taking in our glossy eyes and dopey smiles. "Oh shit, you're right."

"Oh, yeah, no, we both took edibles," I chuckled. I went to stand up again, and my hands pulled at the cuffs. "We also maybe lost the keys."

Collins glanced around the room, closing his eyes in exasperation and sighing after a moment. He walked across the room to the nightstand next to me, picking up a small silver key. "You mean this one?"

"Hey, you found it!" Nikki exclaimed happily.

Collins just reached up to uncuff me, and I sighed in relief when my arms came down and I could roll my shoulders out.

I jumped up out of bed, and Collins and Will called out in protest, turning away.

"Woah, dude, warning next time!"

"I can fully see your dick man!"

"Oops, I just gotta put my pants—" I cut myself off, remembering my pants had been the start of this, and started cackling again. Nikki ran to her closet and tossed me a pair of sweats I quickly pulled on. Nikki and I sat next to each other on the bed and faced Collins and Will standing in front of us with crossed arms, waiting for an explanation.

"Alright, now start from the beginning," Collins demanded, staring down at us like stern parents admonishing their kids.

"So, uh, remember when I told you I was gonna ask someone to hook up with me?" Nikki asked Collins.

His eyes widened. "Oh shit, you meant *James?*" He turned to me. "And you said yes?"

I just nodded my head, letting Nikki control the narrative.

"Hold on, wait, what?" Will interjected.

"A few weeks ago, Nikki told me she was gonna ask someone to hook up with her, but she didn't tell me she'd actually done it. Or that she was going to ask fucking James of all people."

"Damn," Will responded, eyebrows high on his forehead.

"I just thought he'd be a good option. I knew he knew what he was doing." She smirked at me before continuing. "And I also knew he would understand me as a demisexual person. So I figured, why not?"

"So it's just casual?" Will asked, brows drawn together.

"Yes," Nikki replied firmly, and my heart sank in my chest. I'd hoped that maybe... maybe she was beginning to change her mind. That tonight had shown her what we could be. But I couldn't expect her to flip a switch just like that.

Maybe she never would feel that way about me, but I would take whatever pieces of her she wanted to give me. Collins watched me carefully, scrutinizing my face, and I looked away. I was too vulnerable in this state for him not to see through me.

"Damn, guys," Will let out a low whistle. "Should you really be fucking while being friends *and* roommates?"

I forced a nonchalant shrug. "What's the problem? I pretty much only do casual, and Nikki just needed to get out of her head and past her writer's block. Why not?"

Collins just looked at me, and I looked away, unable to hold his stare. I felt like he could see through me, tell how I was really feeling, and I wasn't ready for that.

Will shook his head, "I mean, you two are adults, you can do what you want. Just don't fuck this up, okay? We have a great thing going here with the four of us."

Nikki just rolled her eyes. "OK, *Dad*. Now can you get out of here? We were kind of in the middle of something." She winked at them and they both shuddered, quickly exiting the room, shutting the door behind them.

Nikki turned back to me, lip between her teeth. "Now, where were we?"

As she prowled back towards me, pushing me back to the bed and pulling my sweats back off, I shoved aside all my emotions and tried focusing only on how she was making my head spin with her wicked mouth.

It worked.

Mostly.

30

James

THE WORDS - CHRISTINA PERRI

COLLINS KNEW. OBVIOUSLY ABOUT Nikki and I having sex. But I meant he knew how I really felt about Nikki. I don't know how he knew, if he'd seen something in my eyes that night he'd found us or what. He hadn't said anything to me about it, but I could see it in the way he watched me when we were all together.

I was extra careful around her now, trying to go back to looking at her the way I had before this all started. But when we were alone, we were usually fucking, I kept trying to show her how good things could be between us if this were real. I just needed to get her to come out with me again, and finally, I had the perfect excuse.

Sasha had invited me and a plus-one to the annual Halloween bash she threw at the bar, invite-only. Collins would be on shift that night, and Will was going to a work party, which he usually never attended, but this year surprised us all when he said he was going.

Which meant it was the perfect opportunity for me to take Nikki to Sasha's party. I'd asked her a few days ago, while we'd been lying in bed after a vigorous round of fucking. And luckily, it hadn't taken too much convincing on my part. Nikki *loved* Halloween and loved dressing up for parties.

I asked Will to drop me off at the bar a little early to help Sasha out with setup, but really, I just wanted to surprise Nikki with my outfit when she showed up at the party later.

I'd winked at her as I walked past her in the living room on our way out the door, my costume in a garment bag. Will dropped me off at the party, telling me not to do anything he wouldn't do, before cackling and driving away. I let myself into the bar, which was currently empty, just a few decorations thrown up on the walls so far.

"Sasha? Where you at?" I shouted.

I didn't get a response, so I went through the door in the back, which was propped open, that lead up to Sasha and Lauren's cozy two-bedroom apartment, the second bedroom being used as storage for all of her photography shit.

They were with a handful of their friends were hanging around the high-top dining room table.

"Ahhh, I guess I found the real party," I called out, tossing my garment bag onto the couch. I didn't know most of them, but they all boisterously welcomed me, already half-drunk. Everyone took a shot, then we all broke apart to go finish getting all the decorations and food set up and get into costume.

I couldn't help myself from smiling giddily as I got dressed. I looked in the mirror, adjusting the sleeves of the long, leather coat. I was gonna be hot as fuck in this and would probably have to take the coat off quickly, but the rest of the outfit would still clue people in to who I was.

I couldn't wait for Nikki to see me in my costume. I was dressed as Captain Hook from the show *Once Upon A Time*, aka Nikki's favorite fictional pirate, and biggest crush. To be fair, I also loved pirates—maybe it was a bisexual thing? I smiled as I took in my reflection, loving the way it looked. Under the pirate coat, I had a red brocade vest over a black button-up. They were both opened up halfway down my chest, revealing a light sprinkling of chest hair.

The shirt under the vest was tucked into the black leather pants, in turn tucked into boots. A black leather belt was slung around my hips, a fake sword hanging from the scabbard. I even got a necklace similar to the one Hook wore, along with two chunky silver rings on my right hand. I added some smudged eye liner as a finishing touch, then held the hook inside the cuff with my left hand.

Honestly, the whole thing turned out pretty great.

By the time I was done and back downstairs in the bar, the party was just getting started, the first few people arriving, music pumping through the speakers. I pulled my phone out to find a text from Nikki saying that she'd be here in twenty. The party is always impressive, mostly so that Sasha has so many friends. I definitely couldn't relate.

I mingled, chatting with different people as I killed time waiting for Nikki to show up. I kept looking towards the door to see if she had arrived, but the song "Monster Mash" came on and everyone cheered in excitement, distracting me for a moment. When I turned back to the door, I caught a flash of a brown pirate costume. I froze, my mouth hanging open, when I saw who it was.

Nikki stood in front of the door, staring back at me, her lips just slightly parted. Her hair was straightened, falling around her shoulder in silky black sheets under a dark brown pirate hat. She wore a long brown leather coat with gold buckles, a brown cross shoulder belt holding a fake sword at her side. A reddish-brown vest was buttoned right under her breasts, over a white button-down pirate shirt, unbuttoned enough to show a drool-worthy amount of cleavage. Brown trousers and brown pirate boots completed the ensemble. And in her hand she was clutching a replica of *the* compass.

Nikki was dressed like fucking Elizabeth Swann. OK, so pirates were *definitely* a bisexual thing. I was already hard just from the sight of her in that costume.

When our eyes met after our mutual perusal, Nikki's pupils were blown as wide as mine probably were. We both devolved into laughter as we made our way towards each other.

"Well, hello there, Miss Swann." I grinned cheekily at her, my eyes unwillingly sliding down to her tits.

"My eyes are up here, *Killian*," Nikki smirked at me as my eyes snapped back to hers.

I shrugged my shoulders as I replied, "Pirate, love."

Nikki bit her lip, eyes sweeping over me again. "Pirate indeed."

I reached out my hand for hers and pulled her into me. I slid my other around her waist, tucking her tightly against me as I lowered my mouth to hers, angling to avoid the pointed tip of her hat. Her free hand sunk into my hair, sighing against my lips as I sought entrance with my tongue.

She let me in, and I groaned softly at the taste of coffee on her tongue. Pulling back just enough to look at me, her eyes traced across my face. "How is it that you look better in eyeliner than me?" she asked incredulously.

"I sincerely doubt that."

She sighed in resignation. "You'll just have to take my word for it."

"I say we're both equally hot in eyeliner."

She huffed a short laugh, "Alright, we'll compromise on that. But seriously James, holy shit. Did you just have a Killian Jones costume lying around that you never told me about?"

"Actually, I bought all the pieces to make it after I asked you to come to the party with me."

Her eyes were warm, that same look I swore I saw in her eyes out in the rain. "Fuck, how are you always so sweet?"

"Don't give me too much credit," I replied, giving her a devilish look. "My intentions were also selfish. I know you're obsessed with him, and I was hoping you'd want to jump my bones in this costume once we got home."

Nikki's eyes went half-lidded as she leaned back in to graze my lips. After a moment I leaned further in to whisper in her ear, "I, like Hook, also enjoy pleasurable activities with a woman on her back." I nipped her ear before pulling away, and she shuddered softly in my arms. Nikki glanced around the room, seeing the door up to Sasha's apartment propped open.

She held my hand, forging ahead and tugging me behind her.

"What are you doing?" I asked.

She didn't respond, just tossing me a cheeky wink over her shoulder and leading me up the stairs. All four of us roommates had come to the party together two years ago, so she'd been here once before and seemed to remember exactly where she was going.

Marching right into the bathroom, Nikki knocked and waited a second before pushing it open. Once she confirmed it was empty, she shut and locked the door, then pushed me up against it.

"Why wait until we get home?" she asked, a wicked glint in her eyes as she leaned in, kissing and biting her way up my neck.

"Fuck, NikNak," I breathed, turning my head to give her better access. "Do you even understand what you do to me?"

"I think I have some idea." Her hand traveled down my chest as she sucked my earlobe into her mouth, squeezing my dick through my pants at the same time. "And this outfit?" She pulled back, eyes lingering at my crotch before lifting back up to meet my gaze. "It's really doing it for me. So I want you to bend me over this bathroom sink and fuck me like a pirate. Do you think you can do that?" she asked innocently, a challenge in her eyes.

I stalked towards her with a growl, grabbing her chin in my hand and kissing her desperately, using my other to take her hat off her head and toss it to the floor. I dropped that hand to her waist, pushing her back until her ass hit the counter.

Breaking away, I shrugged my pirate coat off, pushing hers down to the floor next before whispering against her lips, "Turn around, drop your pants, and bend over for me, darling."

She shuddered, closing her eyes in pleasure, kissing me once more, briefly but deeply, before following directions. She turned around, and I watched in the mirror over her shoulder as she unbuttoned the pants, shoving them down her legs. I stopped her hands when they got just past her ass.

She looked questioningly at me in the mirror, but I ignored her. My eyes drifted down to see the small patch of curls covering her pussy, framed by the vest held open by her hips. "God, I can't wait to feel that pussy squeezing every drop out of me, darling." Nikki whined, her chest heaving as she stared back at me in the mirror. I put my hand on her back, gently pushing her forward over the counter. Taking the hint, Nikki bent over, draping her arms on either side of the sink.

I stepped to the side of Nikki, so she could watch in the mirror as I unzipped my pants, and pulled my cock out, leaving myself otherwise fully dressed. Nikki rubbed her thighs together, watching me hungrily as I gave myself a few strokes. I pulled my wallet out of my pocket to grab a condom and rolled it on before stepping back behind her. Flipping her vest up over her back, I finally got a good look at her, on full display for me.

The pants were tight around her thighs, holding them together so she couldn't spread her legs. I grabbed her ass cheeks, kneading into them as I spread her open. I groaned at the sight of her pussy, already glistening with wetness. Dropping to my knees, I opened my mouth against her pussy, eating her out from behind. Nikki moaned, pushing back into me as I sucked her clit into my mouth.

She whined as I pulled away, and I chuckled darkly. "I'm not making you come with my mouth, at least not right now. I need my cock inside you right now."

"Yes, please, James, I need you." My heart surged at her words, and my hands shook as I grabbed her hip in one hand, using my other to direct myself into her. We sighed in unison as I finally entered her.

"Are you gonna be quiet for me, NikNak? I don't want to share your noises with anyone else." I leaned forward, pressing my back against hers as I made eye contact with her in the mirror. She was biting down on her lip so hard it was turning white as she nodded her head frantically.

"Good. I'm gonna fuck you hard and fast, darling, so hold on."

She closed her eyes, letting her head drop forward, whining softly as I slammed into her. I just hoped no one could hear us over the loud music thumping through the building. My eyes were locked onto her bouncing tits in the mirror, and I watched as they jiggled every time my hips slammed into her ass. Her quiet, bitten-off noises spurred me on even more.

I was already close, and I might have felt embarrassed about that if I couldn't tell that Nikki was already just as far gone as I was.

"Fuck," I grunted. "I'm gonna come, Nikki. I need you to come with me."

"I'm so close," she whined.

I leaned forward again, pressing my chest against her back so I could slide my hand around her hip and down to where we were joined. I pulled out, leaving just the head of my cock inside her. She cried out in protest, but before she could even get any words out, I slammed back into, pinching her clit at the same time.

Nikki buried her face against her arm, biting down to keep herself quiet as she convulsed around my dick. Her orgasm set mine off, and I slammed my eyes shut, clenching my teeth to keep from yelling out as I pulsed into her.

We stayed in that position, panting as we caught our breath on the come-down. I gently pulled out of her, wincing at the loss of her heat. I tossed the condom in the trash. I found a package of flushable wipes and used them to clean up Nikki and then myself. My eyes stayed on her as we both got dressed again. She turned around to look at me, a soft smile on her lips.

I grinned back, planting a kiss on the back of her hand, trying not to die from cuteness overload when she blushed at the gesture. I found it equal parts adorable and hilarious, seeing as I'd just been balls deep inside of her.

We rejoined the party and hung out for another hour before calling it quits. We'd been finding ways to touch each other all night, and I wasn't done with her yet—and I had a feeling she felt the same. When we got home, I tugged her to my room.

Falling into bed again, we made out for what felt like hours. I could have stayed there, wrapped up in her for eternity if she'd let me. This time when we had sex, it felt different. It was missionary, and it was slow, and deep, and passionate. It didn't feel like fucking, but like making love. And afterwards, when she fell asleep in my arms instead of going back to her own room, I let myself believe—if only for a moment—that just maybe, Nikki could love me back.

31

NIKKI

Whatever dream I was having, I didn't want it to end. I was warm and cozy, someone's body wrapped around mine. I snuggled in closer, breathing deep and slow. I opened my eyes to see—

Wait, where the fuck was I? I slowly looked around at the unfamiliar view. It only took a moment before realizing that I was in James's room and it was James wrapped around me. I must have just fallen asleep in here last night. My heart rate picked up as I realized that this was the first time I'd ever spent the night with someone. That was *not* part of the plan. That was not what people who were having casual sex did. Spending the night is what people with feelings for each other did, and that wasn't me and James.

Right?

I needed to get out of here. As quietly as possible, I slipped out from under James's arm. Gathering my costume up, I threw the white shirt over my head and snuck out the door, shutting it softly behind me and tiptoed as quickly as I could back to my room.

I leaned against the door, eyes closed as I tried to calm down. My eyes snapped open when I felt my phone vibrating in my hand. Lucy's name flashed across the screen and my hands tightened on the phone.

I could feel the anxiety building in my chest and I debated letting it go to voicemail and deal with it later, but that wasn't fair to them. Swiping to answer, I brought the phone up to my ear.

"Hey," I answered the phone, voice strained.

"Hi, love. Just wanted to call and check in since there's just one month left! How is the writing going?"

I swallowed down the lump in my throat, feeling like there was a weight sitting on my chest as I thought about my writing. I knew it was the day after Halloween, so that meant it was November first, but my brain couldn't compute that it meant there was only one month left to write an entire book.

"Yeah," I lied through my ass, too embarrassed to tell her I still hadn't written basically anything. "Yeah, it's great!"

"Oh good," Lucy responded, sighing in relief. "I knew you could do it!" I gripped the phone tighter, the anxiety and guilt of being a failure and a liar suffocating me. My breaths were coming shorter, and I knew I needed to end this call before I had a full-on panic attack.

"I actually was doing an early morning writing session, and I don't want to lose my momentum, so I'm gonna get back to it!" I was a terrible, terrible person, lying to my agent like this.

"OK, I'll let you go. I'm so proud of you." Their voice was warm and kind, and I wanted to die.

"Thanks, Lucy! Talk later!" I hung up the call before they could respond, drowning in my own shame. I got in bed, curling up on my side and pulling the blankets up to my chin. I was scrolling on my phone, but I didn't even know what I was looking at. I should be sitting at my desk and pulling whatever words out of myself that I could, but all I could do was lie here and stare blankly at my phone while my brain screamed at me to do something, anything productive. Screamed at me that I was a fraud, and a liar, and a failure, and an awful person.

I don't know how long I been berating myself when I heard a soft knock at my door. I clicked my phone off so that it wouldn't accidentally make any noise, staying perfectly still so whoever it was would think I was asleep and go away.

"Nikki?" James's voice floated to me through the door, and I could hear his concern, even muted through the door. My heart twinged, reminding me that I was a shitty person in even more ways. I'd snuck out of his bed without a word, and he probably just wanted to make sure I was ok. It wasn't his fault I crossed the boundary we'd set from the beginning, to not let it be anything more than physical. I closed my eyes, taking a deep breath to try and center myself enough to answer the door and pretend everything was OK.

Getting out of bed, I walked over and opened my door just enough for him to see me through the opening.

"Hey." I smiled, but I didn't think it quite reached my eyes.

"Hey." His brows were drawn together as he scanned all over my face. "Is everything OK? I woke up and you were gone."

"Oh yeah." I waved a dismissive hand. "Sorry about that, I didn't mean to fall asleep in there. Woke up super early and came back to my room when I realized." He tried to hide the devastation in his eyes, but I still saw it. My grip tightened on the door as I tried to keep from breaking down.

"Are we... good?" he asked hesitantly.

"Of course!" I responded with forced brightness, "I just realized today is November first so it's time for me to really buckle down on this draft."

"Oh, OK." His shoulders dropped in relief. "So you'll just let me know the next time you want to meet up?"

"Actually, I think we can probably call it, now." I felt like I was ripping my own heart out as I said the words, but I knew it was time. "I really appreciate all the help! But I really gotta focus on the writing now."

The more I spoke, the more the light in his eyes dimmed.

"Yeah, no, I get it." James smiled weakly at me. "Glad I could help." He turned around without another word, walking back to his room.

I don't think I'd ever hated myself more.

I closed the door and let my head fall against it as the tears started to fall. I gasped in shuddering breaths, trying to calm my breathing, trying not to have a panic attack for the second time this morning.

I crawled back in my bed, lifting my phone back up to keep scrolling. Everything was going wrong. I'd ruined my friendship with James, I still had no book to show for it, and I'd fallen back into my habit of lying to everyone around me because I couldn't face my own failings.

It was times like these that made me wish I didn't have to do this anymore. Not that I wanted to kill myself or anything, but like I just wanted to hit pause on existing for a while. Fade into nothingness for a few weeks or months until everything that was making me feel so overwhelmed that I couldn't function had passed.

I knew that wasn't possible, so instead I stayed in bed, scrolling without seeing what I was looking at while my brain told me what a shitty person I was.

Honestly, I deserved it.

32

NIKKI

JENNY - STUDIO KILLERS

A FEW DAYS HAD passed since Lucy called, and I'd barely written anything. I felt numb to every feeling besides exhaustion. I did my best to push through it though, because I had no choice. I could *not* miss this deadline. The problem was that I felt like everything was wrong with the plot of my book.

I no longer feel stuck with the sex scenes, but every time I sat down to try and write, it just felt... wrong. My main characters had zero chemistry with each other, and no matter how much I sat and thought about how to fix it, nothing was working. I didn't know what to do. How could

I write a romance with zero chemistry? But I didn't have the time or capacity to start over from scratch, which sent me into another panic spiral.

I was sitting at my desk now, pulling at my greasy hair. My eyes felt like they were full of sand for how little sleep and how much screen time I'd had the past few days. I was so frustrated I wanted to cry, but I was too numb even for that.

Someone knocked on the door. I debated ignoring them, but decided to be a big girl and get up to answer it. Swinging the door open, I came face-to-face with James. I hungrily took in the sight of him, trying to resist the urge to grab his shirt and pull him further into the room, fucking away everything I was feeling. But another part of me wanted to slam the door in his face and curl into a ball and never get up again.

Scanning over him I noted the circles under his eyes, his facial hair more grown out than usual. He looked as terrible as I felt.

"Hey." His voice was quiet. His brows furrowed as he looked me over as well. "How are you doing?"

I cleared my throat, shrugging. "Fine. Just trying to get this book written."

James nodded his head. We both stood there awkwardly, not looking at each other as the tension stretched between us. I felt my anxiety stealing the breath from my lungs. I couldn't do this. I couldn't stand here and share space with him like I didn't want to pull him into my arms and lose myself in his body. I needed to end this.

"Well, I should get—"

"I want to do this for real."

We spoke at the same time, and my words died on my tongue as I registered what he said.

"What?" The word fell out of my mouth as my heart seized in my chest.

"This. You and me." James's words were firmer now, his back straightening as he spoke. "I want to be with you for real, Nikki. We've been friends for years, I think you're amazing, and the sex with us is the best I've ever had in my life. I think we could be so good together, and I think you know that, too. We've both been miserable this past week. Why are we fighting this?"

"I don't..." I shook my head, not knowing what to say.

"Please." He grabbed one of my hands in his, and I watched numbly as he cradled it lovingly between his own. "I miss you." He was pleading now, his eyes glistening. "You can't tell me you don't feel it, too. I know you didn't always, I know I used to be alone in these feelings, but hasn't that changed?"

"What do you mean?"

"You really had no idea?"

"No idea about what?"

James gave me a devastatingly sad smile. "Nikki, I love you. I've been in love with you probably since the day I met you."

I was shaking my head before he even began speaking, pulling my hand out of his grasp. "No, no, we're just friends." I couldn't stomach the look of absolute devastation on his face as I pulled away from him, and I looked to the ground. But what the fuck? He was in love with me? What was he talking about? This wasn't how things were supposed to go, this wasn't the plan. He was the one who told me he didn't want a relationship! This plan was perfect because we knew we wouldn't develop feelings for each other, but he was in love with me the whole time?

It was all too much. I was so behind on this book, I was about to lose my dream, my career, my livelihood. I could barely function, and I just needed everything to go back to the way it had been.

No. No, I couldn't do this.

"James, what are you doing? We both knew exactly what this was, what it was supposed to be."

James swallowed hard, and I watched the muscles in his neck move, unable to look him in the eyes. "I'm sick of living my life too scared to ask for what I want. Too afraid to rock the boat and demand more for myself. So this is me telling you that I am in love with you, and I want to be with you. For real. No lessons, no friends-with-benefits, no whatever the fuck this has been. We're perfect for each other, and you know it." His voice was fierce and I felt like I couldn't breathe.

"James, stop."

"I thought... I thought you felt it, too." I couldn't stomach the look of devastation on his face, but I also knew I couldn't give him what he wanted.

I knew what I had to do. "I appreciate you being willing to help me, but that's all this ever was. And now, you're nothing but a distraction." My voice got louder and angrier as I spoke, unable to stop myself from spiraling. "You're the reason I'm so behind. I got caught up in our lessons because you kept pushing me for more, and now everything is at risk. I just... I need you to stop. We are friends and nothing more, and I need you to just leave me alone so I can finish this book and save my career."

Before he could say anything else, before I could see the look my words could put on his face, I slammed the door shut on him. As the quiet echoed around me, the tears slipped down my cheeks. I wrapped my arms around myself, gasping in air that didn't seem to be filling my lungs. I crawled in bed, curling up on my side as my tears soaked the pillow beneath me.

When had everything gotten so fucked up?

Nikki

A WEEK HAD PASSED, the worst week of my life. After letting myself wallow for the rest of the day after James and I talked, I forced myself to get back to writing, but it was like pulling teeth.

And then, two days later, James texted the group chat to let us know he was moving out. His text had sent me spiraling all over again.

It was all my fault. I had ruined *everything*. Our friendship, my book, the apartment. But I couldn't fix it. I couldn't fix *any* of it. I didn't know how, and I didn't have the time. So I continued ignoring Will and Collins every time they tried to talk to me and ask me what happened. I only left my bedroom when absolutely necessary. I hadn't even responded to any of Noah's messages.

But then yesterday, as I had sat staring at my document trying to get the main characters to give me *something*, a conversation popped into my head between the female character and her best friend who was trying to help the love interest fall in love with her.

And that was when everything clicked.

The reason the main characters had no chemistry was because they weren't right for each other. The main character and *her best friend* were the ones who were in love.

In a manic fugue, I started the book over almost from scratch. But this time, the main character and her best friend fall in love. And it was... fuck, it was perfect. It might be the best book I had written yet, even if it was rushed. It would need a lot of work in editing, but that was future Nikki's problem.

Powering through the draft was the only thing keeping the depressive episode I could feel looming at bay. And I was powering through it. I'd gotten through the first act just between yesterday and today.

Even now I was planted at my desk, barely looking up from the screen to to eat or drink or take care of personal hygiene.

Suddenly, there was a knock at my door. I ignored it, going back to the screen in front of me. I didn't even have the energy to tell whoever it was to go away.

But then the door opened, and Will and Collins came into my room. Begrudgingly, I turned in my chair to glare at them.

"What is it?" I asked sharply.

They looked at me with a range of concern and pity that made me uncomfortable, and I shifted in my chair.

Finally, Will spoke. "We're worried about you, Nikki."

"You haven't left your room in a week," Collins said.

I scowled at them. "I'm drafting."

Will shook his head and Collins crossed his arms over his chest as they both stared me down. I couldn't look at them, focused instead on my hands in my lap and picking at the skin around my fingernails. Will came forward, sitting on the edge of my bed.

"I think sometimes you forget I've known you half your life." He gave me a half smile. "I know sometimes you get in the zone, but this... I've never seen you like this."

I sighed. "Listen, I know you guys mean well, but really, I'm fine."

"So we're just not gonna talk about what the fuck happened with you and James?" Collins asked, his brow raised. I flinched when I heard James's name, and prayed they hadn't noticed. But based on the look they exchanged, I wasn't that lucky.

"You guys were doing fine. You went to a fucking Halloween party together! And then all of a sudden, James just up and moves out? What the hell happened?"

"I don't know, OK?" I finally snapped. It was just all too much. "James was..." I swallowed, my voice cracking on his name. "James was a mistake. We shouldn't have fucked around, and now here we are, finding out. I'm sorry." I looked down, my own words hollowing out my chest. Calling James a mistake made my heart hurt for reasons I didn't have the capacity to figure out at the moment. "But right now, I need to finish this fucking book. Just give me time, ok?"

They looked at each other again before nodding their heads and moving to leave. My shoulders dropped and I forced a smile as they shuffled out of my room, making me promise to actually talk with them once the book was turned in. I lied through my teeth that I would. As soon as they shut my door behind them, my smile dropped.

I turned back to the computer, brushing away the tears rolling down my face so I could get back to work.

33

NIKKI

NUMB LITTLE BUG - EM BEIHOLD

I TURNED IN THE book in on November thirtieth. I should have been ecstatic, but all I felt was numb. I was sure it was terrible, and was certain I'd be getting a call from my editor telling me exactly that once she finished reading through it. After hitting send, I curled back up into a ball in bed, pulling the blankets up over myself and ignored Collins and Will when they tried to talk to me.

I didn't want to talk to anyone.

34

James

No One Can Fix Me - Frawley

"Knock, knock!"

The words came to me through a haze, and I looked up from the computer. I was in the manager's office at The Sleepy Siren working on... well, to be honest, I wasn't quite sure. I'd been trying to read this report for half an hour now, but I couldn't get my brain to focus.

I hadn't been sleeping much, and last night I think I got less than two hours. I was barely functioning, and the stress had caused a flare-up of my chronic gastritis. I could go months without even remembering I had it, until something triggered it. But I'd been living at a base level of nausea for weeks now, throwing up almost daily. Zofran had become my best friend.

Belatedly, I remembered that someone wanting to come in was the reason I'd looked up in the first place, and I croaked out a response to enter. The door opened, revealing the hesitant faces of Will and Collins. They looked around the office, and I realized this was their first time in here. They'd come to visit me at the bar once or twice since I moved out, but hadn't gotten all the way back to the office.

"Nice digs," Collins said, dropping into one of the other chairs. Will nodded along in agreement as he sat in the other chair.

"Thanks."

"Still enjoying the new position?" Will asked.

"God, yes," I responded through a huffed laugh. Honestly, it was probably the only thing getting me through. If I had to be out on the floor dealing with customers while I nursed my broken heart, I don't know what I would have done. I glanced at them curiously, wondering if they were here to talk to me about Nikki.

I hadn't wanted to move out, not really, I just couldn't stomach bumping into Nikki around the apartment. Not after pouring my heart out to her, only to have her literally slam the door in my face.

I don't know what the fuck I had been thinking. I should have just kept my mouth shut. Accepted whatever pieces of herself Nikki was willing to give me, instead of pushing her for more. Especially when I *knew* she was under so much stress. I'd fucked it all up, and it was only right that I remove myself from the equation.

After all, they had all known each other longer. The guys were always going to take Nikki's side, as they should.

"That's good." Will nodded his head encouragingly at me.

"We miss you, man," Collins suddenly burst out, and I blinked in surprise.

Will smacked his arm. "Dude, I thought we were gonna be cool?"

Collins just brushed him off. "I know, but fuck, this is all so stupid!" He turned to me, leaning forward earnestly. "I don't know what happened between you and Nikki. She won't talk to us. But I know you'll figure it out eventually. Just move back in, OK?"

I was already shaking my head before he'd even finished speaking. "I can't, man."

"Why not?" Will asked, seeming to give up on whatever plan they'd had. "What happened?"

I swallowed, unsure if I should tell them. If Nikki hadn't said anything, maybe she didn't want them to know. I looked down, picking at the chipping nail polish on my fingers. I needed to repaint them. Maybe a fun winter color this time. Fake it till you make it, right?

I decided to be honest. They'd find out eventually, and it wasn't like things were ever going to go back to the way they were. "I told her I was in love with her, and she told me I was just a distraction." I kept my gaze down as I spoke, unable to handle whatever pitying expressions I'm sure they were trying to give me.

I was pathetic.

"Bullshit." My head snapped up. Collins was shaking his head at me.

"Excuse me?"

"No, not that you're in love with her, I knew that." He waved a dismissive hand at me, and my cheeks pinkened.

"Was I really that obvious?" I asked sheepishly. Collins and Will looked at each other, and I buried my face in my hands.

"Hey." Will put a hand on my shoulder. "There's nothing wrong with being down bad." He and Collins laughed as I groaned, dropping my head back.

"There is when she doesn't love me back!"

"See, *that's* what's bullshit, man. Nikki is totally in love with you," Collins said.

My heart wanted to believe him. But I couldn't let myself go through this heartbreak again. I shook my head.

"You're wrong. She doesn't care about me. At least, not in that way."

"She's just overwhelmed, and stressed. You should see her—she's doing even worse than you." I ached at his words, hating the idea of her in pain, even still.

"She gets like this sometimes, when everything around her is just too much and she shuts down. You just need to be patient with her. She'll come around," Will said.

"No," I stated firmly. "I know you guys mean well, but just—I can't, OK?" I hated the way my voice cracked on the words. "I can't move back in and be near her, knowing she doesn't love me back. I never should have said yes to sleeping with her in the first place, but if I didn't do it, she would have found someone else and I couldn't let her do that. I couldn't let her be vulnerable in that way with a stranger. With someone who wouldn't give her the respect and the care she deserved."

"Fuck, man, you really are gone for her, aren't you?" Collins sounded surprised, and I realized that while he knew I loved her, he probably didn't understand the depths of that love.

I looked down to my hands again. "I love her more than anything. That's why I can't come back."

They were quiet then, giving me space while I collected myself. I'm glad they weren't pushing anymore, but it also made it worse. I wasn't just losing Nikki, I was losing them, too. Sure, they would try to keep touch with me, but I knew that eventually time and space would come between us and we'd drift apart.

My heartbreak would be threefold.

"Will you at least tell us where you're staying?" Will asked, and I finally looked back up to them.

I flicked my eyes up to the ceiling. "In Sasha and Lauren's spare room. At least until I can find a more permanent place to stay. I promise, I'll come get the rest of my stuff once I have somewhere to take it."

"Dude, shut up," Collins interjected. "You're coming back eventually. Just give it some time."

I didn't respond.

"Alright, I guess we'll let you get back to work. But James?" I looked up as Will spoke. "You're our friend. You're not losing any of us. You got that? It would take a lot more than this to be rid of us."

They each pulled me into a hug before leaving, and I slumped back into my chair.

God, I wished he was right.

35

NIKKI

I WAS LYING IN bed in the dark when my door banged open. I didn't turn to look at whoever it was, assuming it was Will or Collins was trying something else to get through to me. But I didn't want to do anything besides wallow in my own pity, missing James and hating myself.

"Goddamn, Nikki, this is depressing as fuck." Noah's voice cuts sharply through the room, footsteps storming towards my window. I sat up in surprise, pulling my blankets up with me and wrapping them around my shoulders as I leaned against my headboard.

"Noah?" My voice croaked out of me, and I cleared my throat before speaking again. "What are you doing here?"

"What do you think I'm doing?" She ripped open the curtains, letting the sunlight stream into the room, slicing into my darkness-adjusted eyeballs.

"Shit, why the fuck did you do that?" I yelled, covering my eyes.

"When you stopped coming to family dinner and didn't answer my texts, I just assumed you were hyperfocusing on drafting and forgot about the world again. That's on me for not being a better sister and checking on you." Noah's voice was matter-of-fact, but she was my twin sister. She couldn't hide the pain underneath her words, and for the first time in weeks I felt something other than apathy. My heart panged at the fact that I'd hurt her by shutting her out.

"I'm sorry," I whispered.

Noah came to sit next to me, pulling me against her until my head rested on her shoulder, gripping my hand tightly in hers. "Thank you." Her response was flat but warm with her particular brand of love. "When Will finally texted me saying he was concerned about you, I came here as quickly as I could."

"I swear, I'm fine," I protested weakly. "Will was just overreacting."

"He was not. You smell terrible, your room is an absolute mess, and you're living in darkness like some vampire from a terrible teen drama."

"Rude," I mumbled.

"But true." I didn't have a response to that. "Here's what's going to happen," Noah forged on, practical as ever. "You are going to take a shower, because you desperately need one, and then we are going to talk about what happened." I was going to argue, but then I caught a whiff of myself and realized just how right she was. I nodded, not having the spoons to respond.

Once I was in the shower, the tears came. Partly for how badly I'd fucked my life up, partly because I didn't realize how badly I'd needed the soothing feeling of hot water pounding into my skin, how badly I'd needed to feel clean.

By the time I got back to my room, it was almost completely clean. The dishes and trash had been removed, dirty clothes put in the hamper, new sheets were on the bed, and random shit that had been scattered around the room neatly lined up on my nightstand, dresser, and desk, waiting for me to put them away wherever they belonged. I began crying again for a different reason.

Without saying a word, I went straight to Noah and squeezing her tightly, feeling like I could breathe again for the first time from the pressure of her arms as they squeezed me back. Noah stood there silently, rocking me in her arms for as long as I needed. I had never felt more grateful to have her in my life.

When I was ready, I pulled back, grabbing a tissue to blow my nose before sitting on the bed, leaving room for her to sit next to me. And then I told her everything. How I had freaked out on James, all the awful things I'd said to him, him moving out.

After I finished speaking, Noah looked at me for a moment, and then she smacked me upside the head. "Ow!" I exclaimed, rubbing the back of my head. "What the fuck was that for?"

"Because you're an idiot."

I dropped my jaw, indignation flaring. "I thought you were here to cheer me up!"

"I never said that. I said I came here to check on you, and obviously not soon enough, because you fucked up big time."

I sighed, "I know. I know you said this idea with James was going to blow up in my face—"

"That's not what I mean," she interrupted me. I furrowed my brows at her. "I mean, you did fuck up with James. But you fucked up by letting him go, not by starting this in the first place."

"But you told me that it was a bad idea. And then you told me to be careful. I thought you *wanted* me to stop hooking up with him."

Noah sighed, looking up at the ceiling like she was praying for patience, before she spoke again. "God, you're so dumb sometimes, Nikki. I told you to be careful because I could tell you were falling in love with him, and I didn't want you to get hurt. I didn't think you were going to go around and hurt James *and* yourself instead."

"What?" I sputtered. "I'm not in love with James!"

"Oh, sweetie." Noah shook her head at me.

I opened my mouth to tell her how wrong she was, but then I thought the weird things I'd been feeling when he did nice things for me. Like pulling me outside so I could be kissed in the rain like I'd always wanted. Remembering my favorite flower so he could bring me a paper one. Dressing up as my favorite fictional man for Halloween.

Oh shit.

"Oh my god, I *am* in love with him!" I exclaimed.

"Fucking finally," Noah muttered, shaking her head at me in exasperation.

"Bitch." I stuck my tongue out at her.

She stuck her tongue back out at me. "Dumbass."

After a moment we burst into laughter, and I fell into her side. Noah slung her arm around my shoulders, pulling me in tighter, and I snaked mine around her waist.

"I've missed you, Nikki," Noah said quietly.

"I know, I'm sorry. I've missed you, too." I sniffled, trying to keep the tears that had begun welling up at bay.

"So tell me, Nikki. Tell me everything, please. I'm your twin, your best friend. You know you can tell me anything, that I *want* you to tell me everything."

And so, I finally did. I told her everything that I had been thinking about and doing. Everything that I had been feeling about myself.

"First of all, you are *not* a terrible person. That is just your brain being an asshole to you, and you need to tell it to fuck off." She gripped my hands, staring into my eyes with a fierce conviction. "You might have made some questionable choices when you were overwhelmed and your fight-or-flight mode was triggered, but that does not make *you* a bad person." I tried to avert her eyes, but she gripped my face between her palms, forcing me to look at her. "Do you understand me?"

I sniffed, shaking my head as much as I could while she still held me. Deep down I knew that, but it was harder to *feel* that.

"Secondly," she continued, "and I hope you'll take this with the love it's intended, but have you thought about going back to therapy? I think it could really help you."

I took a deep breath, wiping the tears from my face, and nodded. "I know. I need to go back. I think... I think maybe letting my ADHD go untreated has triggered a depressive episode. And I need help."

Noah hugged me tight. "I'm proud of you," she murmured into my ear. "Another piece of advice, take it or leave it, but maybe you should try meds again? Only if you want to, of course. But last time you gave up after the first try. It doesn't often happen for people the first time, and if you want to give it a try, you gotta stick with it until you're sure. Only if that's what you want."

I did want to try again. And this time, I would actually follow through.

"I'm here for you in whatever ways I can be, you know that, right?" I nodded my head, and she held me for a long time, letting me cry it out and take all the reassurance from her that I needed.

Finally, I pulled away, turning to grab a tissue from my nightstand and blow my nose.

"So." Noah's voice had me snapping my gaze back to her. "What's the plan?"

"Plan?" I asked, my face scrunched in confusion.

Noah rolled her eyes. "Your plan to get James back, obviously."

"Oh." I deflated. "I think it's too late. I don't think he wants anything to do with me, and I don't blame him. Not after the way I spoke to him."

Noah was already shaking her head before I finished speaking. "No, Nikki. That man is *gone* for you. You just need to tell him how you feel. Shit, you're a romance author! You know how a grand gesture works. Get your shit together." She tsked at me, and I laughed through a watery smile.

"You think so? You think he could forgive me?"

"I *know* he would."

For the first time, I felt hope rising in my chest. Maybe I could still fix things. Maybe, just maybe, for once in my life I could get everything I wanted. Everything my brain tried to tell me I didn't deserve.

Noah stayed with me another hour, helping me plan my grand gesture. After she left, I felt lighter than I had since the last time I'd been in James's arms. Seriously, how did I not see how hard I'd fallen for him?

I waited in the living room for Will and Collins to get home. They'd left before Noah came to give us some privacy, though Collins, of course, called conspiracy theory on Noah even being real.

As soon as they walked in the door and saw me sitting on the couch, they ran to me and scooped me up into a three-way hug.

"There's our girl!" Collins exclaimed.

Will looked like he was on the verge of tears himself as he squeezed my hand. "Welcome back, Nikki."

I looked up, blinking the tears back in. Even if these were happy tears, I'd cried enough today already. I pulled away from them, taking a deep breath.

"So, I want to get James back." I smiled as they whooped and hollered, relieved to know they seemed to want us to be together, too. "And I need your help."

36

James

ORDINARY - ALEX WARREN

"JAMES?" SASHA PUSHED THE door open and peeked her head in. I was lying in bed, scrolling on my phone and trying not to think about Nikki. I wasn't doing a very good job of it.

I sat up. There was a twinkle in her eye that had me suspicious. "What is it?" I asked hesitantly.

"You have a visitor." Sasha grinned at me. "I'll be down in the office, give you guys some privacy."

My heart leapt in my throat. It couldn't be... could it? Sasha left the door open for me before heading down-stairs, but I sat frozen, heart pounding. God, I wanted it to be her. Finally I gathered myself and walked out into the living room.

Nikki.

Fuck, I had missed her so much. Just the sight of her was equal measures a balm to my soul and a sharp pain that had me feeling like I couldn't breathe.

She was sitting on the edge of the couch, leg bouncing, fingers twining around each other as she chewed on her lip. She was wearing that damn lemon dress, and my heart hurt at how beautiful she looked.

There was a flare of something in her eyes as she looked at me, making me want to be hopeful. But I wouldn't let myself. Not yet. As much as I was overjoyed to see her, the last thing she had said to me before slamming a door in my face echoed in my head. *You're nothing but a distraction.*

But fuck if I didn't still love this woman with every fiber of my being.

"Nikki," I breathed her name.

She stood up to meet me as I slowly moved towards her, coming to a stop a few feet away. She gave me a tentative smile. "Hey, James."

"What are you doing here?" My gut clenched as she flinched at my words. But I needed to be careful here. I had no idea why she'd come to see me. For all I knew, she just wanted to tell me off some more.

She seemed to falter at my words, before steeling herself and speaking. "I need to apologize to you."

I still refused to get ahead of myself. Not until I truly knew what she was getting at. But I nodded my head, stepping further into the living room, and sat in the loveseat catty-corner to the couch. Nikki seemed relieved, sitting back down and angling towards me so our knees brushed. The slit in her dress exposed her leg halfway up her thigh, leaving her knee bare. I fought the chills that wanted to run through my body at the touch, as innocent as it was. Her skin on mine would always make me feel something, no matter the context.

I forced myself to look away from her thigh, my mouth going dry with the sight. "I'm listening." My words were quiet. Not unkind, but still reserved.

I watched her as she swallowed, wanting nothing more than the trace the motion of her throat with my fingers, with my tongue.

"I first need to say that I'm so sorry." Tears were already welling at her lashes, and I forced myself not to lean forward and brush them away with my fingers. "I was horrible to you, and there is no excuse for all the things I said. I was overwhelmed and spiraling, and my reaction was to lash out and shut down. I never want to hurt you, but that's exactly what I did. And I hurt myself, too." She let out a humorless chuckle.

"I promise, I will do better at regulating my emotions. The truth is, I'd already been barreling towards a depressive episode, and everything happening was just making it worse, but I didn't want to acknowledge it, so I just shoved it down. But I'm going to go back to therapy. I'm going to work on myself. I want to be better. I want to have the tools to express myself, to help myself in those moments."

"That's great, Nikki." I gave her a soft smile, and she looked relieved. Like she thought I could truly hate her. As if I ever could.

"I'm sorry for the things I said to you." She closed her eyes, looking down in shame. "For slamming the door in your face. I wasn't just overwhelmed, I was also terrified."

"You were scared? Of me? Nikki, just because you don't love me back—"

"Oh, god no," she rushed out. "No, James, I was never scared *of* you. I was scared of what I *feel* for you. You know I'm not good with change, and I was scared of what admitting my feelings would mean."

Finally, I dared to let myself have a shred of hope. "What you feel for... me?"

"I have something to show you." Nikki picked up the binder sitting on the table. I hadn't even noticed it, my eyes only for her. She handed it to me, and I took it, glancing up at her in confusion. Opening it up, I saw that it was her book.

"You finished it!" Despite everything, my first reaction was to smile at her. "I'm so proud of you!" She beamed back at me at my words, and my heart soared. God, I had missed her so much.

"Read the dedication."

I looked down, flipping to the page.

For James. Not only my best friend, but my greatest love. This book, this love story is for you. For us. Thank you for loving me.

I sucked in a fortifying breath as I closed the binder, setting it back on the table before looking up at her. Nikki shot me a wobbly smile as she slid to her knees in front of me, taking my hands in hers.

"I love you, James. I'm in love with you. I'm sorry it took me so long to really see you, to understand my own feelings. As a romance author, there are still so many things about love that I'm not good at. But I want to be. I want to learn, and love, and grow with you. I write words for a living, but no words could ever truly express just what you mean to me. You're my favorite person in this world, and I want to love you the way you deserve to be loved." She paused, looking unsure and vulnerable. "Is that something you want, too?"

I couldn't speak, my throat clogged with emotion. Instead, I grabbed her face in my hands and pulled her towards me to smash my mouth against hers.

Finally.

We both groaned into the kiss, melting into each other. As my tongue wrapped around hers, I felt settled for the first time since that door had shut in my face. This was where I was always meant to be.

We only pulled apart when we had no choice but to breathe, and I rested my forehead against hers as we caught our breath.

"I love you so much, Nikki. Thank you for apologizing. I forgive you. I don't ever want to be without you."

Nikki burst into sobs, rushing forward until she was sitting on my lap, arms wrapped around me, sobbing into my shoulder. I held her back just as tight, burying my face in her hair and soaking in her warmth, rocking her back and forth as I rubbed soothing circles into her back.

Eventually, she pulled away, sniffling. "Does this mean you'll move back in?" She gave me that crooked smile, and I couldn't help myself from leaning forward and capturing her mouth in another kiss, this one shorter but no less passionate.

"You're never getting rid of me again."

"Good."

We didn't come back up for air again for a long time after that.

EPILOGUE

COME TO ME – GOO GOO DOLLS

"HEY, THAT WAS MINE!" Robyn snipped at Alex, attempting to take the drink out of his hand, but he knocked back the glass of champagne before she could.

"You had one in each hand. I assumed one of them was for me." Alex shrugged, motioning to the drink in her other hand.

Robyn snorted. "Why would I grab you a drink, dumb-ass? You're perfectly capable of getting your own. Plus, it's an open bar. Of course I'm gonna double-fist it."

I pinched the bridge of my nose, shaking my head. But I couldn't stop the grin spreading on my face.

"Guess that means I'm just helping the youths." Alex shrugged.

"How is you stealing my drink 'helping the youths'?"

"The more I drink the less alcohol there is for the children?"

Robyn rolled her eyes. "Dude, you just stole that from Phoebe Buffay." Alex winked before sauntering away, Robyn trailing after him, needling him with more insults.

My heart was full as I looked around this room filled with all the people I loved. Well, everyone besides Collins, who said he'd have a surprise for us when he got here later.

Someone came up behind me, snaking an arm around my waist and planting a kiss on the top of my head. I turned in James's arms, wrapping my hands around the back of his neck.

I tilted my face up, and he leaned down to plant a sweet kiss on my lips. "And how are you feeling on your big day?"

I grinned up at him. "Well, now that the singing is over and that beast of a book is finally out in the world and no longer trying to kill me? I'm feeling great." I dropped my arms to turn back around and look out at the room, sighing as I rested my head back against his chest.

His arms wrapped around my middle, pulling me against him. I wrapped my arms over his, and he began gently swaying me back and forth. Tonight was the launch party for my third book, and I couldn't be more relieved that I was here. After the way I had finished the first draft finally, I thought Lucy was going to come back and tell me how terrible it was and that they'd hated it.

But they'd said how much they loved it, how much it made them feel, and that it was a fantastic start. And to be honest, once it had gone through thorough editing, I finally felt like it was a book I could be proud of, maybe even some of my best writing yet.

And now, here we were nine months later, and it was out in the world.

I caught Noah making her way towards me with a regretful smile. She held out her arms, pulling me into a hug. "I'm so sorry! The hospital called, and they need me to come in. But I am so, so proud of you, Nikki!"

"It's ok, go be a superhero and save children or whatever." I waved dismissively at her.

"Thank you, I love you." She planted a kiss on my cheek, and I did the same to hers. My parents came next, saying they were too old to stay out this late, which was Mom's way of saying she and Dad were peopled out.

I hugged them goodbye, then turned back to the party of all our friends—and in the case of Will, a co-worker. To the shock of all of us, he had brought his work rival Allison, with whom he'd had a love-hate thing that had finally turned to love. She was across the room chatting with Robyn, while Will brought shots over to me and James for the three of us to knock back together.

The front door opened in front of us, a tall silhouette blocked by the sun filled the doorway.

"Collins!"

"You'll never believe who you just missed."

"Where's the present you said you were bringing?"

We all spoke at once, while Collins slowly stepped in the door, angled to the side, hiding something behind himself.

"I said *surprise*, not present," he told us.

"Ok, whatever you want to call it," I said, waving dismissively. "Just show us what it is!"

Collins took a deep breath and stepped inside, swinging something large around in front of himself. My eyes went wide at the baby car seat.

"Is there... is there a human child in there?" I stuttered. Collins gave me a *what the fuck?* look, and I shrugged in defense. "Hey, you can't blame me for asking."

"You—" Collins had his finger pointing at me but then he stopped, thinking about it. "OK, yeah, fair."

I was fully prepared for him for him to be pranking us somehow, when he revealed an *actual* human child. I pointed down at them in shock, "Whose child is this?"

Collins shifted on his feet. "She was left at the station as a safe surrender."

"Ohhhh, OK, phew" I said in relief. "I thought you were gonna say she's your daughter."

Collins hesitated, and my eyes grew wide. "Holy shit, Collins, is this your daughter?"

"Nikki, James, Will, meet my daughter, Rose."

We looked at each other, then at Collins, with matching questions of disbelief.

He explained in a rush, "When she was dropped off at the station, there was a letter attached to her car seat. Her mother dropped her off there because she knew I worked at the station. She said I'm the father. It's that one-night stand I had thought would be something more that I had about ten months ago, remember?" He turned to James, who looked confused for a second before realization seemed to dawn on his face.

I gasped again, covering my mouth with my hands. "Holy shit, Collins, you're actually a father!"

ACKNOWLEDGEMENTS

I can't believe we're actually here! There were many times when I thought I would never be able to write another book again. Authors are not kidding when they talk about how hard it is to write book two. So I want to start it off by thanking past Emily for pushing through instead of giving up like I wanted to do many, many times over the past two years.

A huge thank you to my editor, Sarah Pesce, for dealing with my chaotic neurosis and ridiculous self-imposed timeline. I could not do this without you! And Valentina for proofreading, I love you!! Thank you to Sarah Estep for always being there for me to bounce problems off of. Thank you Jeannie Choe and Kristen Jennings for hanging out and helping me get words down. Thank you to Andrea Andersen for helping me perfect my favorite chapter of this book, because writing high idiots in love is just such a fun time. Thank you Leanne Schwartz and Jeannie

Choe also for helping me with the blurb! And a shoutout to my entire SoCal romance author community! I'm so lucky to be surrounded by so many incredibly wonderful and talented human beings.

Thank you to my roommates, Hannah and Christiana, for being my brainstorming partners and putting up with me! I couldn't ask for better roommates, or better friends. Thank you Christiana for helping me map out this entire series, and build the playlist! And Hannah for drawing me the cutest sticker for The Sleepy Siren! Thank you Kaitlyn for redoing my author branding, and also just being one of my favorite people! I'm so lucky to have you in my life!

Thank you to my parents for being my biggest supporters, always. And thank you Mom for spending the past two years flying over the country with me for events and for being so supportive you read my books even when I ask you not to, lol. I love you.

Thank you to Gabby for delivering me the comCom cover of my dreams! And all of my artists: Tina, Snowfall, and of course the loml, Sophie! You all brought my characters to life so beautifully, and I cannot thank you all enough! And of course, thank you to Heartbound Bookshop for being so wonderful and support of me and my books!

Thank you to my beta/hype team! Caitlin, Katie, Kae, Vicki, and Emily, I appreciate you all so much! Thank you as well to everyone who has shown interest and support for me and my books! Your enthusiasm and support is what motivates me to keep going. All I've ever wanted with my stories is to help other people feel seen, and I hope I succeeded in that.

ABOUT THE AUTHOR

Emily B. Rose grew up addicted to storytelling in all its forms, and always knew she would have a career in something creative. With a bachelor's degree in creative writing, she settled on books as her favorite form of storytelling, though you will still find her glued to the TV watching her favorite sitcom or nerdy movie series, or belting show tunes in her apartment (to the annoyance of her cats). California born and raised, she can be found wherever the closest beach or bookstore is, or curled up at home trying to convince her cats to cuddle with her 24/7.

Emily is a proudly fat, demibisexual, ADHD woman who wants her stories to reflect people often ignored, especially in love stories. She hopes her books will make people feel less alone, and affirm that everyone deserves the love story of their choosing.

Connect Online

www.authoremilybrose.com
@ ♪ @emilybrosewrites

9 7 9 8 9 8 8 4 8 3 6 4 9